BEYOND

Worth uh' Dance

Novel story by
JOSEPH FLOWERS

ISBNs

979-8-9865261-4-0 Paperback

979-8-9865261-5-7 Epub

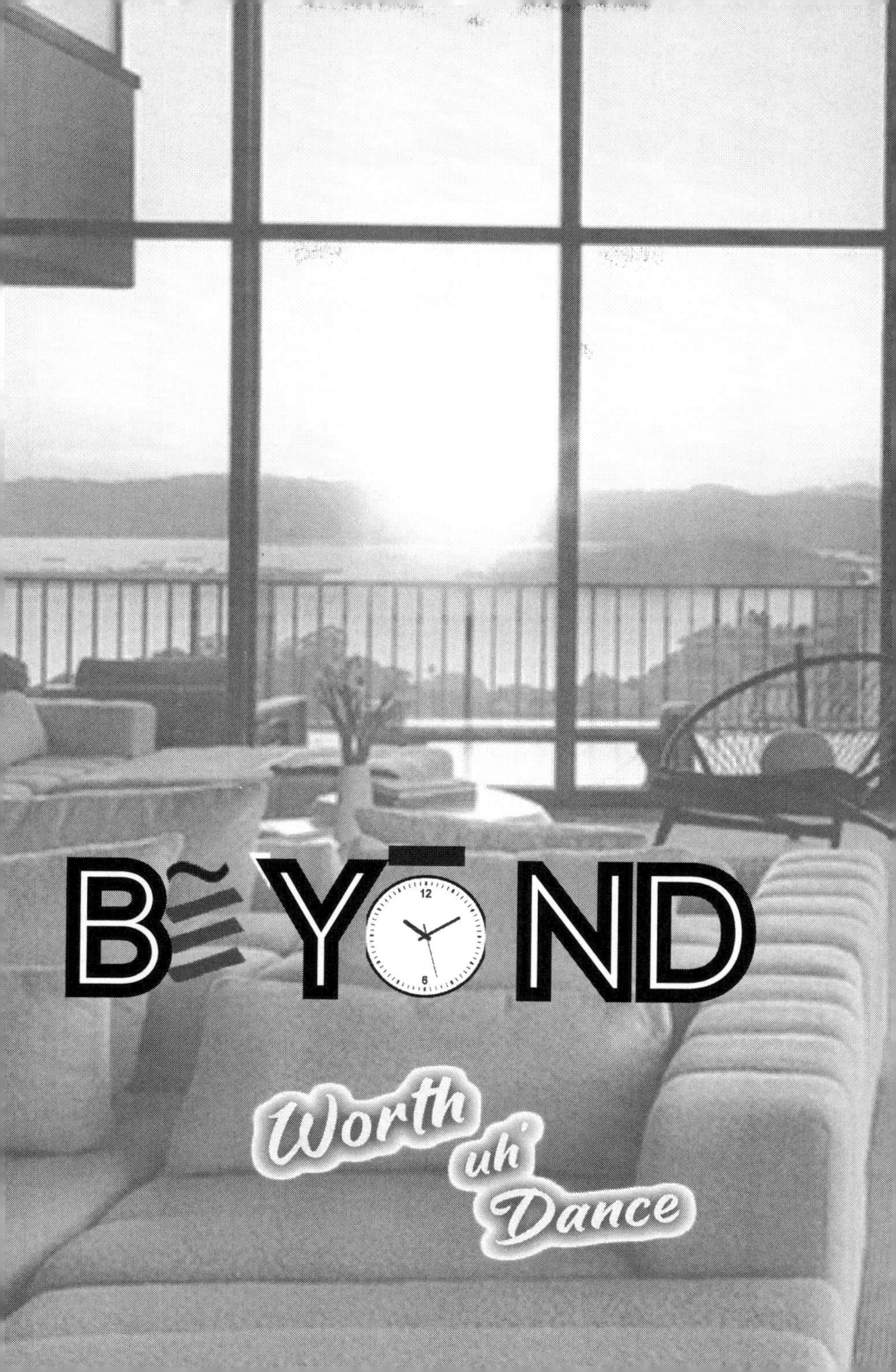
BEYOND
Worth uh' Dance

This novel is dedicated to:

To a hidden smile of mines, always had my best of intrest. It's only a taste of my intuitions, utmost and thanks much to a bestest, the streets that raised these thoughts, and our Bay Area's next of breeds.- it's okay to agree to disagree; like uh' knock spot uh' feature wit few hundred yards in play.

Acknowledgments

The highest of honors and praises up above to the heavenly my father- God, you have continued with pouring blessings upon me to excel with an open intellect; I'll keep mindful of the needs with strive being the best of human spirited I'm capable of.

And thanks upon my entire family/ both sides. My Mother, Father Grandparents, Nieces , cousins, nephews, uncles and aunties, brothers N- sisters. Without you, I wonder where or how might my life had oxygen. And my "best friend" who holds my inner peace- and keeps me grounded- know I'm appreciative` thanks for noticing.

My neighborhoods I grew up in and the deepest trenches of Oakland. The best is yet seen. House Reps worldwide, know I'm mindful of the outreach!

Xtra thanks for distribution services, that's Urban life, Rapbay, streaming platforms, for providing room of sharing these thoughts to filter, I am honored to have the support of yours, as always. Those who purchased any books of mines, thanks and much luv.

The Govenor
aka "The Gov"

Prologue

Greetings readers,

Thanks much for providing me this opportunity to share these thoughts-- your energy and time believe that I do not take for granted. The series was a gripping fun journey writing, I woulda never forfeited it. And honestly, i'm just getting started to know my craftsmanship and aggressively looking to introduce other forms of street urban lit. The stories are the daily hood ups N- downs, trill life -that's what it is. Although, the dramas are the works of fiction comprised of possessions of authenticity. Simply put, "OTD" Off The Dribble series part.2 it's

"BEYOND worth uh' dance " let's get to it.

They doing lap dances
tossin' Rock Stars by stares.

CHAPTER

1

They say it's cheaper biting a bullet sometimes than spitting one, and I'm not about to argue about the differences of opinions; it's facts not fiction. Yet these folks out here on this other side of the Bridge don't in hindsights have any practical realities about life, it's amazing the shackles they indirectly utilize. But okay. It's the wealthiest county surrounding our Bay Area. "I wonder why?" now I'm learning. They hustling under the radar. Welcome to the Land of the braves, they doing lap dances tossin' Rock Stars by Stares while sipping X.O Outta the arch of mittens stand still! Unlike the typical who deviates, before lunch hour I dialed "Omega Star" my ride or die; Good work. Who's always ready for the deepest levels the game prescribes. And today it's visiting she pose ta' slide through- boy, I'm praying she's not dry cappin, and solo-bolo, riding alone. Yeah, I'mm Uh' find out what it don't. "Ms. Bubble Butt." I whispered underneath my breath.

They about to get their opportunities to have an eye fulls, I'm almost certain it's game thieving going on in those visiting booths. This about to determine the fragrance they rocking behind tents. If I'm lucky, might have something for "Ms. Jessica Jackson" and the attorney at Dream Corps. Fresh offa the barz uh' "Class Action Suit." Let those eyes answer the horn underneath the tented windows of "Ms. Bubble Butt." I'll know soonest.

"Mr. Maxwell Pixar, you have a visitor in room B. your half hour starts once you enter the open doors." The floor deputy announces over the units intercom, i'm nervous as hell, thinking to myself' "Please let that be Ol' Omega Star. As I mumbled to myself out loud while putting the finishing dabs on my well-kept silky waves, dipping so hard you coulda' pushed a wave runner jet ski on those oceans. Just got finished doing my thousand push-ups an hour ago. Lotioned up those bedroom abs, looking like uh'runway model ready for ah' Drew House commercial. Her little jukebox gone be knocking da' most I hinted. OK Max, it's about dat time fa' rise and shine, grabbing my plastic from today's lunch bread, squirted a pinch of Jergens body lotion right in that thang, stay ready you ain't gotta get ready. It's about to get jiggy; lil momma Ms. Omega and I ain't laid eyes on each other going on six months. She's Jawsn, bluffin of practicing celibacy since going on New Year's, I'm like Aliiht ! But good. Lucky for us, yeah right! But I'mm give her the benefit of the doubts why knock her for having herself ah' New Year's resolution.

Life's precious, if she's keeping that vault shut there's rewards for exercising pause buttons.. That's uh good thang, I'm dancing in circles finding myself pacing for oxygen, preparing for this visit. My body's processing my desires of what if Omega read my intentions over the telephone, during our last conversation yesterday. And she comes fully equipped to serenade like uh' hungry piranha, anxious to run that, we rockin.' Okay showtime, as I enters the visiting room, I'm greeted by lil momma; looking so aggressively sexy. I gleamed over her voluptuous figure while searching for a proper ice breaker to set the vibe on non-orthodox relaxations, but intimate zones. Within seconds I found her body language peering through the glass and onto my lap. Woooh! And she was flyin so-lo-bo-low. I almost lost my mind, but I caught myself. "Clam it down Maxwell," hold tight now do not spill the whisky." Sparks flew, but I didn't lose contentious as I hadn't wanted appearing to overly excited, but Damn! Everything was in the right places, and I mean everything from her French toes to her milky pulps. As I moved to be seated without losing contact of her tender thighs; which spoke of a different volume than her tone of voice. Explicit with a drift of force of nature, as I perceived something more promising about her everytime her hips adjusted positions. Only thing that I could say was, "Damn, you about to make this hard on the both us!" After she'd thoroughly undressed me without even speaking a single awe. Somehow, I managed to lever what was obvious to become subtle, but yet futile. Hell, I completely forgot about "Ms. Bubble Butt" dancing to its own rhythm behind the tents, as my unopposed attention had me rethinking the dial of her ring finger, leaving my thoughts frozen, flirting with outlandish possibilities. Not excluding the reasons for her deciding to wear a button down pullover, four sizes to big, perfect timing and place. As I declared my gauge, slightly harassing, leaving the options for her to splash without causing huge waves, registering to the sound bites of the alarms that not only mines, which most men with any kinda taste buds vigorously answers to.

"You always outshine the sunshine don't you?" I boldly reclaimed, interrupting our silence. "Omega Star"almost sorta paraphrased in thoughts; of what appeared she was likely about to say, upon me drawing a smile outta her. But instead, her reactions were a hidden fetish that I overwhelming considered were somehow mines. Bang! She unleashed opening her wardo upper garment, and two jaw breakers nurseries outta nowhere stared out at attention saving the day, aimed centered into my dilated pupils. I knew we were on a time limit, it was just my recreational of reflexes. "Thirty minutes only gon' torture you." Omega whispered barely growling, nearly almost inaudible to be unheard aloud, to avoid any disturbance, from alerting the units other inmates, while not aware of any aspects of her 'co-pilot flying above us. "Ms. Bubble Butt." Quickly she closed her blinds before giving any opportunities to become fantasize with a blip.

"Do as you please lil mama," I blushed upon her actions. Revealing the Jergens outta my lunch wrappings, as I positioned it on the table Just letting her know, I came ready to party please don't stop with da' music Let's dance! While despite the facts we could be likely under surveillance from hidden eyes of Ms. Bubble Butt. Yet we still hadn't done nothing to dodge off any routine ops from peering. I wasn't about to interrupt our vibe, though. They'd just gotta do some paperwork, I'm already in the hole drenched, they can't woop my ass! At best, what I might lose lil pod time. "And!" But I wasn't about to floss to hard though, bringing out the hammer, ya da' mean. In my opinion why jeopardize this lap dance lil moma going hamm! And doing the fool, closing her eyes trying find something, I ought know what she'd misplaced. But boy, she was active like uh' knock with a strobe light. "Do what you do lil mama." I posed, inviting our good time. "Okay, I'm almost there." Omega Star pleaded just as quietly and casual. You wouldn't of thought in a million light years we weren't someplace other than a Hilton 5-Star Palace, given how peaceful she purported seated opposite the windowpanes. "Is it almost noon yet,?" I quizzed, but she didn't answer.

"Have you found whatever you're looking for?" again she was wide eyed, but not unattached. This kinda' stare, I'll fess up, it's not for everyone to glean or it could spread like uh' bad dream. She paraded on as if she wasn't able to speak, with an agenda likely about to be going viral, that's if my insinuations of the unknown were correct, "Ms. Bubble Butt" was dancing in its own corner.

Out of nowhere Omega responded with da' sexiest facial features and silent cries, which spoke of a different measure, letting out huffs and puffs, catching her breath before speaking.

"Woooh! why did you need something?" Mustering that violet look in her eyes that matched my next unspoken thoughts. "I ought lap dance to busy tossin' Rock Stars by glares."

"Daddy you proud of me?" She fought not to ask. I obnoxiously insisted on her to give da' time, but she respectfully declined to answer. Like she always does, brandishing that faithful coined signature proceeding forward with lines of her own questions while unstudied of the time.

"You thought I wouldn't answer the horn if you dialed?" I inquired further while she defended her position—I filtered.

"You never disappoints anytime you know margins on the line, that's what I admire about you Omega." Quickly I urged her to explain herself. Which upon I like to believe that I'm a multitasker, was busy focused on the greater substance, the dinner not the desert. Luckily, I hadn't lost my thoughts while placing my heels into the visiting booth, during the same breaths clutching ahold of my ghetto card- of which I've been eagerly waiting for the right time to draw. Letting the four levels characters fully soak, reclining with my hustler sponge out, active and attentive. Didn't even have to apply the Jergens and scored that touch down. If that's not winning! Before getting out what was on my tongue the deputy inside our living quarters floor panel yells, "Mr.Pixar your times up sir!" Now mind you I'm locked under the radars for possession of a concealed weapon charges, and like always they got me wrapped up on parole since way when. As the bailiff yells, times up Mr. Pixar, I'm like damn time surely fly's when you're handling some business. I answered.

"Aliiht, about to wrap it up." I motioned into the living units quarters corridors given lil' mama the final opportunity to finish collecting her thoughts.

"You know it's in your court now, make your next move our best news!" Omega, ferociously insisted while she dipped from her seat, getting ready to spin off, I ensured her. "I'mma keep 20/20 visions over those thongs, I like bout it bout chic's know how to answer, they score!" Brandishing that twinkling sensitive heart stare which signified, "only in due time!" But she wasn't lost for words. Insisting, "You know to love Omega means only you're sure of yourself." Those heels were born idle for Lamborghinis, pulling up into Fleetwood cribs, fully decored tucked somewhere off da' coast in a lavish spread. Unleashing her golden wink, implying. You just watch, I'mm bring you da' bitness! Was the way she ended our visitation. Then leaving my response surveying her imaginations at the deepest of its realms, leaning on the edge of my angelicas, yet seizing her up and down as a body language expert "Blanca Cobbs" woulda. Before concluding um! Feeling some other kind of way." Although speechless, I didn't know whether if I needed responding to her pleasing rhetoricalness, my internal instincts commanded. But sometimes the best is unsaid. I vowed for the rebounds looking the other way to the days ahead noticing provisional roads to the Oscars doesn't always require you to reveal the routes veered. There's a ecstasy finding a balance often with a gentle hold. I ought know about you, but I'm delighted from life's daily struggles and those whom be rooting for you, whether you won or lost., If they bottled that up into a single fragrance titled "Notice" presented by Golden for Men and Maxwell for women, you think that'll fly off the shelves?

*Measured thoughts have
residuals we'd be jealous of
for a lifetime!*

CHAPTER

2

Fast forward two years later I'm floating down the walkways when I overheard my name yelled over the yard's loud intercom. How it sounded, I knew it was a blessings in the skies. "Maxwell Pixar report now to

R&R "Receiving and release." Praying to God they'd received my writ of habeas corpus. It's a petition you file once you've fully exhausted your direct appeal often are the long shots, denied even without benefits of the doubts. And surest nuff, it was Alameda County Sheriff's there for transporting me back for a courts order, which was unforeseen. I looked upon the heavens above, like ol' Lord thank you; you have no idea how happy that I'd been pulled outta the stack of thousands. I found the strength to gather prepared for the upsets, while looking forward to the better days ahead. As I dressed out in a Orange Jumpsuit, white stripes and my worker kicks, the kinda shoes envied by the other inmates. Yeah, those sneakers. The thoughts of freedom paced my mind at such a grand capacity, I wasn't abled of focusing on anything other. And guess who came for transporting me today? The one and only correctional officer "Miss Vasquez" her and anthor deputy, Mr. Adams. He was well liked by the hood and block boys on the yard. Soonest he seen me, laughter immediately commenced.

"Hey what's poppin Maxwell?"

"Ain't to much, just been exercising this ol' body and soul preparing for the days aboard."

"Beyond the cute and picky and or the high siddy." As I proceeded..

"Yeah, I'm hipped." Adams conversated on.

"That's good you've been conditioning yourself, letting your time work ta' ya' benefits. You looking chizzed up, like a T-bone steak. You about to bring some recreation when you hit the streets of Oakland huh, Max?"

"Please believe dat! I assured as Miss Vasquez studied on in disbelief at my latest edition - physical frame that I've worked overtime with during these last ninety days. Watching my diet, carbs and banging out my thousand push-ups daily. Taking only Sundays off no prisoners otherwise, on my A-game. She fought and held out as long as she could, but when Adams released those handcuffs my back arms made a perfect horseshoe. Her eyes twinkled like thirty two inch Cadillac Vogue tires, two-ta-one dilations. Almost certain she required a restroom run. Her pants gotta' doing they own dance. She asked Adams for five quick minutes, when she returned, it was impossible not to notice the difference which screamed through her facial features, the same gestures configured with my dialects, while she blew in and out deep sighs of relief, before whispering softly.

"How's you these days Mr. Pixar?" Which she always addressed me with following a matching hidden smile underneath. I "likewise" held the same platonic stares.

"Better than yesterday, but under circumstances you know I'm not complaining "Miss V." in you?" Her tasty response had me near thinking- bet not say.

"Every time you speak Mr. Pixar you never cease to amaze!! Dat's what's up! I looked over "directly into her sexy brown eyes without miscue. Then dialed, intunded. "You noticed the drawl." She wasted but uh' second until her commits flaunted.

"Your choices of words, and that unique but distinct bite, you making this harder and harder. And that six pack, you need to keep uh' shirt on round me playing before you get yourself rebooked on an assault, possession of another deadly weapon."

"Uh, what! Is dat' right Miss V." I fired! Well you know I've always had a strong desire for flexin, not fully aware of her motives. Although, not wanting to ignore what was partly visible. Her concealed reactions to my actions, had meet eye to eye, you know it's bound when other folks notice ones google stares. That still wasn't enough suppressing that hard work certainly pays off. In addition i found within myself a little sense of energy from her intimidations. I ain't gotta' clue why, but I'm attracted to women who knows how to handle well under pressure. But never may have the full answers honestly to those question, and please don't let her have the slightest bowlegs, or can dance and hold a tune. On the other hand I'm being respectful. My mother have always raised her baby toh be well mannered. Anything other is a stunt against the dribbles of life's drastic measures. I fought ignoring my mirrored gaze. But the qualities of hers was hard to reason with fo' sho. Miss Vasquez she could get the bitness on national TV at prime time- daily rocking that wavey ass hair do. Yeah! And I'm hoping she's taking a judicial notice. They say money comes without instructions, I respectfully tend to disagree, as every vehicle that's manufactured is equipped with a drivers manual with plates. Look, it's okay! You ain't gotta pay me no mind. I'm knowledgeable of self-resistance and the thoughts of avoiding being periphery's. Which may explain a majority of overlooked opportunities that has presented itself. Her out-of-nowhere response caught both us off guard.

"Um, I hope you find better things for you to focus on in your spare time. As this appears; nor look like your type of lifestyle hon'." And before I could even comment, Adams butted into our conversations. Like ta' got choked.

"We gotta be getting on the road ahead of this lunch hour traffic jam. It'll be four-ish in the afternoon or better until we reach San Leandro (which by the way is two towns between Dublin and Oakland). In a playful, but serious dial, lil mama, Miss Vasquez surprised us again. Splashin' out, "Adams, how's it every time you notice that I'm interested with anything you gotta put your thoughts in play. Who ask you for your wishes and or advice!" Then she coned her eyes while weighing down on those tender hips and thighs, before ordering "Come on let's go."

Adams hesitated then clapped, as he'd should. "That would be time-plus-time-and-a-half. Alameda County ain't paying like dat, so due what you do!" He phrased, with a hidden smile underneath; well recognized, which suggested, make decisions quietly and outta sight, but not outta mind. Hell, I fell out laughing the rest of the entire trip, leaving the best unsaid. I woke up about an hour later. Just the smell of that Golden Gate saltwater brought back old tasteful thoughts of when I once was free to leave and go as I pleased. After passing up the Lake, on our way back through Grand Ave. "Boy" uh' tear slipped the eye for old time sake, needing anything other than some good   old school Columbian gold weed, two white Zig-Zags, a bottle of cold Moet, and my do not disturb sign in effect!

Back on the yard in Santa Rita, it was dreadful, that's putting it lightly. This facility gets on my damn nerves. Although; the homies were looking out best ways they knew making life comfortable as they oughta! Upon I arrived it was Max, you need anything. Socks, covers, fresh threads, whatever I needed was on deck. My Ponta "Nutty" from the deep trenches of East Oakland kept the best smoke and didn't mind extending his arms to offer his latest strains. Providing a place of sanity, taking a break releasing my mind off court, but it was only a band aid. Look-uh-here! As I rose to find lil mama Miss Vasquez dipping through swinging more Azz than a little bit, droppin lugs on me like it was cool fa uh' young dude ta' rock something. But the stakes were way to steep for diving out there. She woulda' had to bite first, cause placing a down payment on a "Maybach" isn't da' least bit cheap. But I can't lie, the thoughts ran through my mind of forgetting about these damn shackles and approaching her as I would any other women out in traffic. Yet, I applied the restraints against the fishing, steppin outta bounds. I have no suggestions how, but she had that "Let freedom ring" written, signed-n-sealed. Ready to be delivered upon instructed. Where, when and how. But instant actions at times doesn't guarantee to have the best results, noticed! Yet, still gauge the rebounds. Without doubt, love promises to hold for another big day! Like you I'm hopeful. With blinders on!

Having faith in God durning the roughest times of need I've found it very therapeutic, versus the desire to keep steering through life without a proper foundation to build upon, sometimes it's heaven sent. I do not under any means pretend otherwise. Who says it hard to believe upon the unseen? Grab the wind. If you still thirsty, which my thoughts are consistent with my favorites journey, go hand in hand, imagine dat! My plank of course, without slipping away, I'mm holler. I won't pivot my responsibilities that's uh' hustler's plea. But I live to answer those reflections beyond the stated poetic phrases. Yet, I'm mindful of the darkest moments, and moved by the fascinations going forward. Given instances likely the fundamentals warrants a modern approach, more finesse improvising. knowledge holds of importance and is a required move, not to adjust its own tune, avoiding the gritting. But utilizing brain power, instead of relying on physical strengths. What I admire has lengthen rewards. As do measured thoughts have residuals we'd be jealous for a lifetime. Study yourself, it'll surprise the best of us. Just by the ability to realize how treacherous and steep one's actual mind is. Not only can probe, but creates, it's enough that'll have you jeer for days. Try halting and listening while opposed to just reacting on impulses, might find yourself sprung from actual sequencing of your own eyelids. Not to say that every action doesn't often deserves a reaction. Only I'm implying most hurdles can be thought through. Almost anything in life, whether good or bad. It holds value to its adventures. You'll have to look under the surface and channel, non-judgmental. Although, it's best safer than sorry. Experiences are to be lessons appreciated versus viewed. "I cain't win for loosing!"

Dreams manifested on the block.

CHAPTER
3

My final sixteen months came and zoomed for paying my debts to society. I paroled back to Oakland, while during my time away, only thing wished for was becoming self-made as an entrepreneur. The hip-hop music game was beginning to take on it's bounce. A primarily forefront was centered in the Bay Area. It was nothing for producing our own musical compact discs. Then releasing full length LP's into urban modern pops music stores. "independently" moving a hundred thousand units at seven to ten bucks per CD and five for cassettes. But you still needed that direct lead in the distribution outlets. There's artist outside of the Bay, from Southern California gained better leverages having major companies in their back yards. But still we found ways of bonding leveling the fields.

Some artist acted quickly who understood those

disadvantages and opportunities early upon. "Maxwell" included. Having acquired relationships beyond the Bay Area, helped expand those visions. Despite we had In-a-minute and City Records, Walter and the very ingenious J.B, The West Coast Don. Mr. Elliot. The streets were on Knock! Fair to say. Too short and his then Road Dogg "Fready Benz" taught the whole Bay Area how to hustle out the trunk, alongside dudes like B-Legit, E-40, Ray Luv, J.T The Bigga Figure, D-Shot, Master P. plus, a host of others underground kingpins. We learned the game and established our market shares. I credit most of Bay Areas underground foot prints upon the real "O.G. Saint Charles," Uncle of the Sick-Wit-Records crew, who cornered and marginalized the aspects of the Bay Area's independent formats, utilized still today. His philosophy and intellect opened our perspectives and insights "world-wide" since the rap game hasn't been nowhere nearly the same. I'll only referee to him as my real hip-hop ponta.

Putting my two's and few's in motion, I hustled my heart out formed a company from the ground built up. Known as "Vogue Tires Entertainment." Kicking my solo career off at a studio out in Richmond, as referred to as "The Zone." which was almost striking distance on feet to Oakland, held famous rap legends "Freaks of Tha Industry" we politicked our moves and grooves reciprocal. Our initial contacts were dynamic, as there, we formed our bounds. I meet one of the realest down-to-earth-brothas ta'graced Planet Earth. As I'll only refer to him as my "real hip hop Ponta." Both of my heels were planted into the streets hood gravel, his was crafted making movies and music. We connected right off the dribble. Notably our relations were placed under the radarz. Because during these fazes of the game Oakland hadn't seen the hoods hiphop side of hustling and grubbing Pedigrees. Filming on the big screens without doubts put punctures between the traps and how Hollywood respects the today's Lorenzo Tate's, Induced by commas and Osmosic postures. Creating a somewhat level playing field, resonating for the hoods to get next to the likes of Jada Pickett Smith's, Queen Latifah's, or the Lisa Clarks attentions, I apologize to you Mr. Tee. As I myself wasn't quit focused, likely to busy captivated with dirty money fast whips and other kinda toes. But I learned quickly the differences of stock, versus living animated going full throttle. Only thing I'll maybe agree to acknowledge, not absent there were errors along the way-ways. If I measured my thoughts before overlooking Excursion Limousines and dance floors I often wonder where would our revolutionary mind state be today? Yeah, I'm posted matching with identical stares. "Implying" Pay attention to what's unsaid, while not letting yesterday's fears determine today's impasses. Yet, determined opposed to others ploy, might decrease possessing Lexus thoughts. Enabling upon to distinguish the B/S from the real. Escaping poverty; overstepping puddles of mud while not tasting the struggles along the way. You'll not likely have the same respect for the trenches-arguably. I'm not speaking from chasing what's between "Smooth girl" spreads. I cain't lie, though there's issues pent up in my thoughts imaginations of the likes of say never mind- which is although, nonerasable. Yet, and I'm okay about pastings of that somebody Intervening happily. But these days I am armored up with two safety hats and sleeping with one on cause at times even tha' notions manifested on the blocks looking to get lucky, in hopes of plotting and preventing a dude playing of his next of moves. Gotta pause and think though, ain't no licking the vessels paint or blowing on the Zeuses amps, Just keeping the beat banging! Cuzz now days if it involves me throwing my interest on the table, bring out da' carpet treatment, white rose petals, plus Platinum settings to hold in place da' chill work, as it'll be no illusions even an NBA referee gone notice precedence on display.

It's the week-end the festival at the Lake. Exciting to the eyes to greet. Baskin Flockin's 31 flavors, Rice fa' life, chocolate, snow, not to mention the hands of exotic historians they forthright belong in our habitat. It doesn't have to be nothing in particular. Just saying. But it's what we do yearly, invite out the best of the best to show up, and out! Similar with Daytona Beach or Spring Bling's. The only differences, it's an Oakland festivity. And they be dancing through from around the globe paying homage and enjoying the finest Cali sunshine we have to offer out in this Bay Area. And boy it be's gleaming! Most be pretending to be single.

That's at least that weekend. But knowing damn well they booked with multiple predispositions in the nest. Still pushing, and not without anything other than Bloomingdale, Sac's Fifth, Nordstrom's flossin sprees on their agendas. A portion often do hit the lotto, including us men. Not to stereotype, but the pave be bombarded no hype, a mirror type reflection of a Miss America's beauty pageant.

The Bay Area's "Maxwell Pixar" arrives and surrounded with a street team full of fine princess, and plenty merchandise for sell. Movie-size posters, and T-shirts. Over the nipples were spruced "No Fishing" on the fronts. The rears, "Maxwell's at Bay." Out front leading the stack, Ms. Omega Star and her dime piece crew packing more flavors than life savers, equal physics in the right places, give uh' take an inch. Put it dis-way, any given day they'd be know for causing wrecks, and that's not isolating traffic jams. And I'm breaking out in fits, just imagining Omega solo gliding threw the lake festivities with a hugging pair of perfectly Madonna fitted stretch pants, need I offer more. Taking over the sidewalks as if City of Oakland issued her, her own personalized permit "signed Omega's walkways only, blinders recommended and permitted!" when I approached the stage, the building went ballistic into an uproar. The town instantly knew a legend was being born. To energize da' crowd, "immediately" I yelled. "Oakland's-in-the-building!" The feedback was offa' the whips, over five thousand people responded at the top of their lungs, today that's about sixty thousand in hindsight. "Hell Yeah!" Then the homie turnt up, got the building even extra hype, echoing his appearances outta nowhere. Women lost their minds bum rushing the stage, fainting breaking out in cold sweats. They little jukeboxes were boiling once he took off his pullover warm up suit, he was every bit of uh' hundred and sixty pounds and that was infact him soaking wet- but cut-up like Bruce Lee, rockin' uh' few thousand in coins of Junk Jewelry, big ol' hollow Nefertiti pieces with matching rings were amongst the glitz and glams the homey sported. Although, in those days any type of jewelry worn you were virtue considered an elite. But the homey was political in content with swagger, hip- hop, yet gangsta-gangsta! You woulda swore uh' swimsuit model just dipped through the building in a G-string getting ready to hit the runway for a Victoria Secret, Fenty, limited edition summer wear. Folks were amped showing their appreciations, top notches fought for closer positions in hopes of snagging a glimpse of the hoods up and rising movie star. My ambitious Ponta yelling out at the top of his lungs.

"Do my ladies run this mutha fo' ya?" and you know that reached nearly kicking a riot off as they answered as surely.

"HELL YEAHH!" The D.J announced on the tables his presence with exquisites writs work.

Appearing out from behind the draped curtains my other homey revealed his motto black ski mask pulled completely down, "Road Glide" yells aloud.

"Now do my niggaz run this mutha fo' ya?" The whole crowd erupted to another level, which warranted for expansion of security. The building went outta control and couldn't be stopped. Ready to take us outta there to the bridge that's when I interrupted from the opposite part of the stages other areas. "Aye Dogg it's on." I wasn't abled to finish out the sentence before those jerks pulled the sound. Damn, I almost let off uh' few shoots from the Glock tucked underneath my Pendleton sweater, I wanted kickin a grandfather clock up their asses. The excuses later given they thought folks lives were at risk and in danger. I listened and quietly had to ask myself. Since when do ops obtain the right to start thinking for oppositions? We ain't in jail, shit we're at the festival of the Lake, that's what's wrong now. We need to ask more questions, instead of being to quick to judge, which appears obsolete.. as if you hadn't known. The standards of ghetto fabulous played right upon itself out. Bottles, garbage cans and gods knows what in you went flying through the air, you woulda thought you were at a circus how much fun it looked from a distance glance, until shots begun ringing out. But it quickly changed its course. Gladly there wasn't anybody seriously injured. Channel 7 news helicopter did everything but land smack right middle into the streets on Lake Shore Drive, snapping flicks and recording the aftereffects. We cruised back through the strip once everybody disappeared just to see how much damage was done to the neighborhood, looked like the Oakland Junk Yard. Philly cigar boxes, liquor bottles, condoms, you name it was everywhere on the streets pave. The next morning was bizarre! As I woke up with a migraine headache, the kind that'll have you crawling in the bed crying "momma." My head was banging and slamming like onyx! hell, I couldn't determine whether not uh' dude was coming or going. However, the evening was a victory. The town was offa' the hinges. Maxwell Pixar became a household name throughout the West Coast, stretching maybe even further.

The taste was not-stop headrushes. V.I.P everywhere, and you know I kept it lit, me and my clique road thicker than Quakerz Oatmeal. Flossin we patent living that phase. While the fame was gained only brought on more differences amongst the non-believers. At times it was difficult to determine those with or against us. But boundaries instituted by the older homies, flushed any speculations from joy riding on our plates.

*My dearest quest gets
amplified as the days go.*

CHAPTER

4

They say when it rains it pours, and I'm posted analyzing it as a running continuous maze of drops. While searching for a higher power. Seeking answers at every direction, looking to avoid the un-sequestered. Out of nowhere received that knock.

"Vogue Tires ENT," was going broke. Lying there fantasizing in hopes of a major recording contract deal to drop outta thin air. It was either hustle, get deeper into the streets, or point seen money gone!

Grannie just alerted my attention to get my mail underneath the dining room table. Almost caught Max off guard.

"You have a letter from a real estate agent, look underneath the dining table." As I'm headed out the front gates, getting ready to drop off this thousand newly freshly printed batch of CD's, of blessings to the hood. I halted! reached to grab the letters, then noticed the agency's logo Century 21, and slide out. But I pondered In deep thoughts.

"Pad my pockets or get at this realtor to find out what steals were on deck. But, I didn't follow

G-mom's instructions, figuring only somebody's looking to sell me a piece of real-estate. Why I hadn't stopped in my tracks, blinded of the facts! And simply thinking, I'll handle that at another time on the rebounds. My dearest mistake. Which gets amplified as the days go. Although, the quest today gets somewhat easier to digest. That's only because utilizing such experience has become of my purpose going forward. I'm aligning now with any signals attuned to finding those lost possessions, for which is my compass of life.

Some things worth more than just money.

CHAPTER

5

It's Thursday afternoon, the sun's beginning to set, which means it's drop top convertible weather. I'm debating if I'mm dial up "Bra, Network" for exchanging whips for the evening. There's a pool party going on across the bay, I've got the direct lines on, suppose to be some top notches invited and interested flyin' in from outta' states. Perfect right, for introducing the area of exotic flavors to Max's new Porsche truck. Freshly polished, I'm feeling relentless today. I've decided not to fade the Jeffery's lounge; that's the downtown number one hang out joint, only thing rocking during the week, and they be doing way too much. But I'mm dip on over the bridge with my campaign *Skird – Bam*!

Now I be damn! As this broads pushing uh' Lexus GS 400, pulls right out in front of my Whip, on Broadway Ave. stomps her breaks, wraps up my front fender. Now the airbags out got me hysterical , I'm just getting outta the slammer. I can't win for loosen! You knowing my parole agent about to be set tripping. As I'm nodding to myself with disbelief. Although, I believed I've done nothing wrong, and driving licensed up. But I'm knowing this investigation gonna require detention regardless for the sorting out the facts. If it ain't one thang it's another. I argued upon myself, before exiting outta my vehicle to survey the damages.

Before you knew it, I'm quizzing the GS Lexus driver who just darted out in front, crashing my vehicle head on! Which now, I'm outta the whip and in investigation mode. Looked like three to four parties exited their vehicle but only one stayed, "the driver." The others took off on foot as I approached the driver for questioning. "You almost lost us both running that sign." While before she could begin to explain with any explanations you know I drilled her, wasn't considering fives, nor moved on the others riding inside the vehicle. The driver was present, and longest she had license with insurance, we were ok in my eyes. As I held my steam from blowing off, cause you know parole officers be playing for keeps in California. I lead on. "Look, I have no doubts you were doing the limits, but you hadn't even second gazed my direction, or simply ignored who was in the right to go first. I'm headed "Southbound" on a green light. You just dashed right out in front of me, then within a glimpse pumps your breaks. Leaving me without any room to stop. Listen, the both of us have damages as these vehicles are repairable, we're still breathing, alive and kicking. I'm not going to worry about your friends who vacated on us. Most importantly, as I insisted with attitude of sincerity. "Not to interrupt, I exclaimed to the Lexus Driver, she begun expressing her position. "This was not solely your fault, as I do acknowledge but do you have any insurance?" As I did not feel the need to answer, but I offered.

"well, yes I do, why do you?" I defensively held my stance, thinking okay. I'm knowing she's not about to try and reverse the liability. While at the same thoughts, looking to avoid involving law officials for obvious reasons. Ya' boy was riding dirty Camillionair style.

On parole, and any slightest of confrontation with police officials almost it's automatic, the results following. In California it's mando arrest. How other states work, I couldn't answer that. But out here! Ask anybody they'll let you know. You may well be smoothly in the right, having done the slightest to nothing wrong, despite your parole officer has the authority and likely will violate you, hold you in custody. No merits whether charges are being brought up against you in a court of law. Hell, they'll indict a flimsy ham sandwich. My contentions if you're prevented from contesting your innocence, you shouldn't be liable for punishment. Similar with if "ones old enough going to war, you're damn surest old enough ordering drinks!" Yet, those are questions, daily goes absent responses. But, is it fair?

"I apologize having asked you this any sooner your name?" She poses. The GS Lexus driver, catching me fully by surprise and off guard.

"Oops, I'm Maxwell Pixar." Forgetting formal introductions of the stigma. Likewise, she held the same answers in stares conveyed. By not having introduced herself, then she extended.

"And I apologize but, I'm. Delishis Gap! Although, Delishis works fine." As I thought, who could disagree at beauty's rare finest. Nothing other than awes. As Ms. Delishis had me under her drastic restraints while we shared our mutual google eye stare downs. Before stopped by, "It's unfortunate, but let's do ourselves justice and hash out our differences between us. We need not to involve any police. We're quite aware of what's required and obligated." But looking over Mis. Juiciness underneath those Spandex's I almost had to ask her if she caused our wreck on purpose. But she wouldn't of understood my taste buds, probably not. And may have likely took it the wrong way. Instead, I looked towards the sky for an answers. Had to say a thank you prayer and ask of God strengths be shined upon me. Who can blame God's creations on man! While withholding my thoughts to avoid sending the wrong signals. "DO YOU" by the artist Neyo begun playing in rotation nonstop in my head. The whole entire time I'm thinking of Omega. And how she'd be devastated if she glimpse wind of any inkling of the thoughts I might have looked in Delishis Plate. As I worked with persistence of retrieving my pocket book out of my vehicle's center divider. Carefully searching my console, while Delishis hunted for hers. And simultaneously our conversations went further than expected to the next level. My uncertainty was in her friends disappearances, hopeful she wasn't about to Houdini before verifying her full identity. Maybe she was inferring along those same lines of inquiries. I paused, studied over my shoulder and seated right there was, you know it. Ms. Delishis Gap.

"Excuse you, who's given you permission of sliding into my whip?" I posed in question, "Yet" not honestly looking for any direct answers, but what followed, I couldn't refuse.

"We're adults, let's handle this at a table for two over a steak and lobster dinner." I fought trying reasoning her intentions, while stopped in mid phrases.

"It's my fault. Regardless whether you have any insurance or not, I wanta make certain what's owed you isn't caught between the yellow tape disputes hon'."

"That's what's up." I politely considered. As she continued stating her position.

"A real woman doesn't avoid her obligations. I'm not going to be satisfied until you're happy. Drive to the nearest Wells Fargo bank." Imagine dat! I contenplated amazed outta' this world.

"Say no More." As I slammed the door looking every bit of optimistic, like. You must be looted up, bouncing into my whip lil mama. But reading Delishis' actions, I halted, and meditated her invaluable conducts leading up into her excepting responsibilities. I wasn't much fearful she'd be disappearing without following through on making good. She was like uh' test of a lifetime, under no other pretense had I understood how women are often several hindsight steps ahead of most men intuitions. They kinda gotta be, In order to stay intuned ahead of the gaps. As I note they'll let us proceed as if we're bringing the noise. Yet holding their hands to the nest, under the storm, just waiting for the right hours where love counts da' most and peek! You ever wonder why us men love you women.

Delishis knew the score the very moment she danced into my "Porsche" and understood her intent well enough to know we shared the same visions. As I pulled into Wells Fargo's drive through, she kinda hesitated. Her looks were paranoid and alarming. I admire how her eyes lit up. To ease her suspiciousness I moved quickly. Redirected my approach by pulling in front, leaving her the room to groom and have no fears withdrawing out uh' loaf without any pressure breathing down her neck while surely it's known, women works are at their best under the heat. But I didn't press-da'-ish! Being she was dressed in Spandex. I handed her my pair of sweatpants outta the hatch. While brandishing non forgettable devious looks, which yelled loudly but silently.

"You to much for T.V. lil mama." She waited not a second before smacking and batting of her eye lids.. um! "Quit hawking me like dat, you makin' me nervous. I'll be right back ok, I promise." As Delishis pushed off, I couldn't help but to look content. Still wasn't enough avoiding my heart slippin' at loves' first sight. As I fought the unforgettable, but our Volume between desire, lust, and taste, had an arc something you'd learn to grow acquainted to. If you vested these basis you know. And it was not only those stretch pants, her body language wasn't any help. Gotta be real, she deserved the next Louis Vuitton, or Prada commercial. Her physique, oh-my-God-look-it-how-she-talked-back. Goosh! Had to pinch myself for her to even gazed Max's direction. Those hips and thighs on her wouldn't spared Jesus eyelids. The grain was da' kind uh' make rice have an attitudes on any given steak day. Well done, have the runways, I'm only guarding the plate! Just looking, was getting full. Strike ah' pose lil mama. "Look-it-dat-meal." Taking over the streets while strutting into the bank, knowing she blocking lane traffic. I wanted, but kept my spar under the warps.

Just as the practitioner ordered, she dipped out looking so bubbly brandishing two envelopes busting out the sides of her seams. Though I wasn't bothered much off the whips damages, nor the loot. My crush was planted on her since her very *initial* words dripped outta her mouth, which melted my unspoken thoughts. I asked myself dang! Why she took almost the whole hour inside the bank- but then again didn't wanta' scare her, which she had to known it's dangerous toting that kinda loochie around open in Oakland public places. But I didn't raise the alarms, held my inferences that's when she looked over and smiled.

"I figured you might appreciate this." Delishis. handed the two Wells envelopes over, they both were stuffed. One had a personal handwritten letter, the ink looked still drippin' to dry, read:

"Lamborghinis keys are at the Broadways Benz dealership waiting for you. I purchased it outta San Francisco, and had it delivered to Oakland on the flat bed. It hasn't been driven. You'll be the first to test out the wheels."

I didn't wanta appear overly excited, as getting money has always been something of a born trait of mines. But she capitalized any deviations of thoughts I hadn't understood about how an imposition women who's interested supposed to properly make her presence acknowledged, versus offering bait. Before opening the letter, I hinched, maybe that's what she was doing taking her time, ordering the Lambo. Yeah, right. I'm not going to believe this until it's in front of my eyes, but yea aliiht! The script went:

"Somethings are better unsaid. But you miss out on what's unknown, rewards or setbacks. Know I have a leisure taste for your type, don't lap me for having versatility. I grew up with my thoughts on Forbes list, but interested in you know, the street kinda' guy that works out regularly, home before the likes of da' moon fades, abled to detect the rise versus the run, doesn't get upset over particularities I find at liberty. Aware how putting himself in valuable thoughts and honestly surprises those around him. Unafraid of Paparazzi's out and about, i'm interested. What I'm offering you is nonrefundable. You in my opinion deserve the best things life has to offer. The reasons I've written you this letter "Max" often at times loves unspeakable. Dial 415-453-0142 ask to speak with Lucy-K. Give her code Delishis, and Maxwell. She's the floor lady working at San Francisco *Luxuries*."

I held my thoughts in check but gritted. "That's how you get at me huh!" Kinda' had an inference we breathe the same contentions. Her , noticing a kings vision." I peered into her eyes for her hidden smile. And couldn't stop there. But didn't say a thing. Only complimented her stares. Maybe to busy studying the two Wells Fargo envelopes. Likely I wouldn't know.

Aliiht. It's good I'mm phone up Miss Lucy-K, I ensured her and instantly begun peeling into those envelopes. Didn't even question the amount. She hadn't struck any suspicious vibes, and beside the dent, the fender bender, wasn't super. Hell for under six bands at best it was fully repairable. Besides gazing over the envelopes, appeared every bit of fourteen stacks. That's just "Off The Dribble" without skating through the wads of cash. "Who's Miss Lucy-K, what she have to speak with me about? Our business is strictly between us two. I'm not interested involving your sidekicks." As I hoped to refute the offer, but not looking to raise any unneeded sensory nods. "No smoke" her commits were satisfying.

"She's a honest friend someone that I lean on for different measures. You'll not find her questionable. That's if you had to reach out to her for any questions about the Lamborghini. "Got you, I'mm follow through and tap in, how sweet of you." Still not fully believing she had that kinda' loot to drop on a Lambo for a person she'd known just uh' few hours. Maybe there's absent pieces surrounding this puzzle. Cause dats billionaire type of shit. And it's only two, maybe three women whom I known in my world in position of splurging like that! Possibly she had a move going on and needed some assistance. But I doubt that. She could sense. Although, it was unmeasured how she was capable of busting a power play for a quarter mill, not thinking nothing of it. Or could I've bumped into a Federal Agent seeking an inside into my infrastructure hefty lifestyle. As these were amongst the several thoughts twerking enlarging through my mind. Forcing me acting outta meticulous terms. "What's wrong Max, you've gotten awfully quiet on me. You have anything to say?" Myself kinda' quivery, but didn't loose the handles.

"Well, I do but I'm looking for the words deserving of your grace." What if Omega finds out, again raced through my mind, faithfully. "You not gone count your funds, at least?" You need not to trust strangers as quickly, do you believe that's wise? "Look who's doing the jawsn. She just supposedly landed a brand new Lambo, for an individual she's only met today, and inquiring my intuitions. Heck, if anything I needed asking her questions. But I didn't raise uh' lid. It's best I hadn't. I'm not the dude gon' put my foot whereas I have a seat, dining out on sushi. Plus, it was very insightful just admiring the distance a persons gauge reaches. I rreplied. "Not in a million years, but you make a valid material notable. Although, I'm fazed for what's in front of me, which is very seldom. Trust. I'm not saying this to score brownie points." I launched that out there for opening up debates, in hopes of learning more about her pedigree's intellects, beyond the streets. Her feedback, this I knew had to be either lobster or steak!

Out of nowhere. "Pull over let's talk." Delishis over aggressively orders just as if I violated a knowingly mandate and required an admonishment, but still had she given one, the wound was broadly incurable. But who wouldn't. I attentively listen for ah' much broader resolution.

"Let's talk, yeah." I heard that! as I begun chewing on my bottom lip, nervous with my thoughts travelling a hundred thousand seconds per minute. You know that kinda I'm-about-to-rock-her-world syndrome. You know men's bold rhetoric! I dribbled to loosen the stares. "Yeah, the beach is just up the way, like going towards the San Leandro Boulevard, It's our very next exit." You driving I'm not complaining. As her arms lifted, motioning to the air, as In response she wasn't opposed to the options I Just proposed. "Say no more lil mama." I nonchalantly volked, while noticing the difference of her mood shifting in my favor, while at the same pace unloosened her bra strap utilizing only my eyes as handles same while driving. Of noxious, I didn't wanta ruin our interval, but those two Wells Fargo envelopes were unrestrictly dialing my fingers at a pace required me peeling into. I counted out twelve stacks. That was only the first envelope, that was enough. Upon As I verred over my shoulder blades searching "Delishis" not for any apparent reasons in particular, only to ask myself "what am I getting myself into." Am I obligated or am I just lucky? We pulled over beachside and sipped our piña coladas and tilted the seats, found ourselves lost in our breakfast, time flew ZOOM!! Involved into a life's journey, comprised full of unanswered questions to date. At least for outsiders looking in perspectives, I'm not the least bit pressed, my visions content.

"What's with you lil mama, you musta' did this on purpose?" As I dished her way. Looking to draw the line.

Delishis just looked the opposite direction to the sky, didn't bother answering, only smiled. Then suggested.

"Max let's getta uh' shower before you drop me off. You must know that I do not wanta leave anything half assed. Anything I do has a purpose. And No I didn't intend for that to happen. You'll be safe, nothing to get hysterical over. You have to trust, I'm an honest woman of integrity. I wouldn't disown, nor avoid my womanly duties and or obligations." How she phrased her comments kinda scared a dude as if there was unfinished business "likely" between us. "That's not what I asked you. I appreciate you were forthcoming with stopping once you noticed having pulled out in front of my whip. But it appears now we've reached uncharted grounds. For self-conscious, I have to ask, are you taking any pills?" which was obvious there were unanswered lingering questions.

"No, I haven't since about two years maybe. How did you know.. bust that?"

"I didn't, you were rough while-ridding, it just popped!" I looked for an excuse, but there wasn't anything she or I coulda' said to defuse what was quite unobjectionable.

" I promise, you need not to be concerned with me, you'll not hear anything outta' me once we depart our ways." I wasn't lured to what if she decided to get lost without guarding the digits. Moreover the experience was a mind blowing event.

"Off The Dribble." Woulda' been disrespectful had we proceeded with our daily lives as if meeting each other had never existed. Somethings are sentimental in value, worth more than money, living and or dying for which most would find likely dearly worthy beholding. Bittersweet and sour, it was *waaay* to much happened between us. Dropping off Delishis was a pressure button that drew blood vessels just thinking about us going our opposite ways. I've prayed before, but never to these extents for answers. I knew my time was running out until having parting ways.

Doing so was a level of the game to which wasn't scripted nor explainable. The looks in her eyes danced buoy anytime that I asked her where she preferred to be dropped off. Her silent response pried into my heart, the wounds are permanent. We finished conversating at the Hilton Marriott, she took an hour in the bathroom freshening up. I wasn't arguing. I dipped out to get us a plate of Hickory Pits' Barbecue, letting her breathe while clearing up some needed mental space genuinely. I almost forgot about the second envelope tucked tightly wrapped in the glove compartment- nor had I opened and examined it. But on the route to scooping our food I peeked, finding she had withdrawn an additional "Eighteen Racks." I'm like how on Gods earth was lil mama able to get that amount outta' that single branch. Could she be an undercover decoy looking to dismantle our family's entire foundation, or setting me up to be ambushed. If that's her objective "why" did she offer her full identity, revealing information about her family and places for doing business, or am I overly undermining my gangsta. Noting I am cheesin' plus, worthiness for landing those thirty bands. But off the hip, for a dingy fender bender "Okay." I am driving a Porsche, as I weighed. But what increased the debts of her diagnosis ? The damages of that amount I questioned. And the "Lambo," if she's not Jawsn, maybe we'll never get those answers. Nor am I about to inquire. Hell, if anything I'm looking to learn her foot works, cause on these blades out this way it's not nearly moving like dat'. I'm knowing better, then again she's beyond stock, and speaking three different languages. Mandarin, Spanish and English. Her DNA traits rang evidence something other about lil mamas make was unknown, that's just gazing from the naked eye views at best. Too looks been known to be deceiving and at times very rewarding. But what I'm opposed. "Forms of prejudgmentals, no one deserves being stereotyped, without justified opportunities to defend those notions.

Delishis had implied her family's business jewelry store which sat downtown Mission District in San Francisco was a distribution outlet for a majority of the diamonds throughout the West Coast Swap Meets. Now, if that's not doing plenty! Gotta' looking at my time wrist work dancing on the wrist, noticing I've been out flossin' over an hour. I'm praying "Delishis" hasn't gotten any creative outta sync-Hercules ideas, but uh' dude put uh' "P.P.I." (*proper-patent-ingenuously*) down something viciously. I woulda' just about betta' couple stacks that she was posted matching gazing far beyond the dribbles.

Let's holler bout it!

CHAPTER

6

Up against the worst of times we learn to adjust, and if you have a significant other, that's where we lean often towards. Which it's typical for most "us" humans. Right? But what I love about the game of life. Women, you're the threads on the Vogue tires. Without you we'd slide right offa the roads; for absence of traction. I found spending majority of my days wrapped in Omega's visions. Although, she'd arrived that I musta hitta' divider in the road. It was written and visuals were vivid. Boldly stamped upon my facial features, requiring answers. But I avoided her questions outta respect. I didn't wanta' deny my reasons for not showing up yesterday. She did not deserve being dishonest with, but "Delishis Gap," she was worth more than that dance! Just saying though. Since we're dealing in truth and honesty. "Let's holler bout-it!" was what I intended on launching.. Instead, I placed myself into her position. And asked, "now wouldn't it be

unreasonable to give her the bad news before the good."
Either way she was getting both because she deserved
that solid rock between uh' hard place. Cain't say it wasn't
difficult washing my hands. As even the strongest of "us"
decides our next and best of moves, paramount under
tough decisions. Although, gotta give credit where's due.
Women approaches are highly way more thought out with
a balanced cause and effective response. Try breaking the
heart of uh' woman's. Boy! That's uh' whole another story
in itself for a different conversation. I'm not ready for,
"But ladies, know it's never on purpose. But sometimes
it's hard ignoring our smiles!" Let's leave that alone." Cuz'
you know women – just saying.

"Babe what's wrong?" Omega asked eagerly wanting
only to help. I didn't know how explaining the slip up
"cash route" between Delishis Gap and myself, noticing
how her questions were distantly warmly placed. I
wondered! "Later's like now, might we get this outta the
way sooner than never. Yet, I yielded my response while
settling upon, "Nothing in particular, just I'm having
infrastructure despairs, pushing about this independent
album, and may have overly invested some funds that
I needed not to." I founded upon myself preparing her
for the anniversary toast with an expensive taste that was
now posted out front. "Delishis Gap" as promised, and
kept! Before pulling in I picked the Lamborghini up at
Oakland's Luxury dealership on 10th and Broadway It
just arrived from the other side of the bridge. Sitting
on stock blades, apricot sprayed, with soft "tangerine"

gut pippins inside. Cleanest of the year. Give uh' damn about the salt displayed, lil mama Delishis- Indeed, was "Beyond worth uh' dance." Exclusive for cuffing season. Which although it was bothersome looking through the gaze of Omegas' bottled pain, She knew something was unstated even without saying. Not that I intended hurting her. "But I be damn! She gone haveta' respect this one, take it on the chin and rise up like uh' real boss lady. Delishis just dropped the sexiest quarter smile that I've ever gleamed my entire life. "And the notion she didn't think nothing of it." Now that's fancy! Still what became between us wasn't imperial enough for me to throw out our landscape we built in minutes time, she offered her undivided assistance and boundary free laser focus. Went on to suggest, "I apologize, but I do not run from itineraries. I chase what completes me, and real picky about the Vitamin D's on my plate." While she held an uncomfortable stare which inferred, "It's your move, what you tryna do." I debated for a second, gathering my thoughts before responding. "You already know." Just maybe what I deserved, favorited her traits. I conveyed within myself. Putting dat in motion, the world is at bay. I honestly wasn't prepared of disarming the keys to the Lambo Miss Delishis Gap scored. But some things the heart has no universal tangible answers, to which most might find profane. "Depends" where your position sits on the laminate and your destination is aimed at the time. Kinda' took quite uh' a while before the opportunity presented itself for us finding our happy medium balance. Soonest as that happen we flourished like ol' mustard seeds.

Delishis heads up, she was in her prime Just getting her feet wet, wasn't into negotiating what she believed in. I'm given it as I found it. She had one of the best struts and always kept in the purest forms. Beyond looks, her presence had me shook! Nothing of her make-up was average. She was fascinating by dancing to her own tunes, and her gene for getting money was phenomenal. How fortunate and in control of her own excellence. Although, I assumed She hid the facts of receiving inheritance as her general reliances, but it was plentiful. I contrive, not that she needed the extra dough, likely was just to keep spare pockets form getting bored. But I doubt anybody around the blocks knew the numbers to the vault, where she hide, what's causing me to wanta' likely J-walk. Lil mama coulda made uh' K-Mart outfit look as if something Valentino would've handmade. She was like that. Well within a league of hers by choice not force, with a luxury mindset for expanding upon our itineraries. I wasn't complaining I almost hadn't notice her pick maybe probably moving just quickly at lightning speed but never utilizing dense thinking. I'd be lying saying anything in opposite. "But she-hada'-bounce!" greasy elbows, detoured on "M" routes. "No movies, McDonalds, or Motel Parking lots." Lucky me, Omega didn't avoid taking her foot shuffles to the streets, attuned into my musical interest. She believed if customers had an opportunity to taste what's on the stores menus before purchasing, both parties benefited. Utilizing those same orients by driving into neighborhood ghettos giving out free CD samples and

t-shirts of Max Pixar's we knew by the time we reached our front porch record companies would be posted out front of our doorsteps eager and ready to offer us a seat at the table. And off to the races we dipped, through every local neighborhood's ghetto. The Bay to Los Angeles we flooded with "Maxwell Pixar" displays. Posters hung and promo gear was distributed to any and everybody we could reach though out the urban hood sights. The record sales increased, local distributors answered our rings, enthused to get that golden opportunity to strike a deal. Without saying I motioned in action parading by eyesight responses. "No thank you." I'm booked lil mama! She like, do you hon. your lost, plus what's over here love starts times two what's on your wrist, anyhows! I couldn't help but notice her gaze never peered from the wrist work which was flooded out in marbles. I'm rocking my Beyond's piece, bracelet and pinky ring worth uh' leisure down payment on a hills front beach spread off in Sri Lanka somewhere. Outta sight outta mind, ta get ya mind right. That's my mechanism if you not woke, you studied wrong chase was drawn. As a hustler and in fact at my best repertoires while up against the ropes. But you knew, Max wasn't fishing. Just kinda' interested what she had to say. It's funny cause Omega always use to get upset with me for paying attention to any other women who flirted at me, which made perfect sense.

Only if I'd known the underliyin' *significance*. Again she was far ahead of the distractions I'm living with right now. They say beauty's in the eyes of the beholder. Interpret that however you wish. She was a classic with da' handles of uh' WNBA Star Guard. And extra, extra, extra thicky! Quit Playing bo-y!

Refocusing my attention on uh' trap in front of me while noticing Lady of smiles, that's what she kinda' struck me as on first Peeks, looking overly ripe and wit da' business. Lettin' her sell it, it's the flavor from the hoods presence got her noise whistling like uh'

Super bowl Referee. But no I hadn't questioned her frisk. She ghetto parks her two-door coup show pice, and then heads towards my direction half naked, stopping traffic switching and throwing Dat-AZZ!! if the law permits- willing uh' spare, dressed in a pair of, I denounce to say, almost near two sizes to tight biker shorts choaking her thighs just right, out of the Ye-Yangz! My goosh, hold tight lil moma.

They say money speaks for itself wouldn't you.

CHAPTER

It's next level twerking on ah' good Saturday. My pager on overflow but I'm breaking speed limits tryna' get to Omega's spot. Those days of me patrolling up and down Foothill East 14th Boulevard it's over. Tenders waiving a dude since that Lamborghini danced through the blocks, they'd forgot how to act, tryna fake kick it. That's out! Then they'll see you with something that's full-fledged they start wit da' noise. Looking to have yours feeling uncomfortable, that's when you find Max floating right past Zapco board knocking. the woofers be signaling turn me down please. Gangster whites gripping on the whip feets hugging da' corners- Old school Chevy darkest blue on the globe, white pimp stripes, baby blue guts, forty-seven thousand O.G. miles clean as the board of health. Leaning skating through like the homies would say, "You know money speaks for itself. After last weekend, I cain't even hit the block without one flocking looking breaking their necks, tryna get me to pull over. Hell you think I'm bitin' no sir, wrong bait! I'm not about to be getting caught loose leaking, not likely. The haters love to gain the upz. And I'm born to avoid the fatal attractions, and I'm not fo' excepting no's for the answers. Gotta adore they optimism though, like dis' one super bad thang outta the hood who seen your boy shining caught a dude off guard, surprised the heck out of me, bravely imposed. "Like, I just gotta dance with you one time. Damn with y' fine chocolate AZZ!" I'm like woooh-where dat materialize from. Looking like, quit playing I know you ain't about to forfeit uh' once and ah' lifetime, I fought not to unload.

"Lil moma if you do not take off your lil sister blouse, you and those watermelons peeking out, looking like you protesting for a penalty. And tha' motions in her hips were doing more than just enough for sustaining my attention and thoughts in position, as I took a second look -reality slapped me. Now I'm just about to pull out from fishing, but she was biting on the line, couldn't help but notice while gazing those track star legs on her knee high, strapped in a pair of leather fire engine red heels, and her feet was pouting out the fronts off the ritard scale. The frostiest promos I've seen in decades. Like she dipped those jokers underneath two buckets of motor oil. Greasier than a "KFC's" meals. OMG. Ain't no sayin' when's da' last visit she's paid a nail salon. And you know those Asian shops on just about every block now days with very affordable prices ain't no excuses for women denying keeping they heels outta scoring positions. And she was thinking about pushing up on my whip, browsing. But I'm playing my hands like, "now, Max, stop dat! Be nice- she's only making friendly conversation. I hoped like the hell those were her intentions. Cause her flabber gassing that's dated! But since we were fishing I went the distance to avoid her cussing me out. Knowing women you have to think ahead, humble yourself while not forfeiting leaving uh' first good impression. Most fumble during initial fast breaks being too greedy. Abandoning they hustle cards for instant rewards. Instead of playing for keeps. "Not saying the

fade`ways aren't sweet." I'm hopeful. But surrendering that Omega's good, good home retreat. No can do, gotta have dat! That's the reason Delishis and I haven't spoken. Despite the Lamborghini was gravy. Although, having warm sheets and covers for tucking you in. Feels way more heart hearty. Those Lambo shoes get cold- and old. "Good-good," hold its heat. That's why I might look, but to find another like "Omega" doubt it. Her heart it'll *forever* never hurt again. "Promise." Before she could reply I'm getting interrupted by rings on my cellphone, blinging off the hook, my initial thoughts were not to answer. But gazing the number from the screen's ID, I noticed "Train Wreck" my cuzzo was dialing through. He would screw up his own wet dreams. But in due respects I couldn't ignore him. Plus, He doesn't mean any harm. He's known going the distance for any of his fam. And Grannie, loves her some Wreck's. Though it's times he gets blitz off that "Old English 800" brewski and-is-nerve-racking. A handful to muster with at times, gotta love his humor though. Everybody has that one family person who's a comedian. Yeah, that's him. On the fourth ring I answered, "Speak on it Wrecks, what's poppin with you?"

"Hey cuzz," he responded. It appeared something was melting at his thoughts, I sensed from the tone and his vibe. As I felt a measure of intensity was underneath weaving. "Maxwell, you know they just scooped up the homey Seven Hundit they raided the hood about uh' half an hour ago."

"Quit playing!" As I answered outta disbelief.

"Say it ain't so. What in the hell!"

I couldn't believe what I just was listening to, thinking to myself, bet it had to do with lil mama off the Sunset strip, that he pushed out with the other day. As I looked for refreshing my lost train of thoughts.

Who? I answered. "Look, Wreck's I'mm dial you back. What's da number you hittin' me from? Never mind, it's in my phone log. Hold tight." This ol' senior citizen in front of my vehicle dancing on her horn she's hysterical. As if I'm blocking lane traffic. "I'm sorry grandma. Damn! I thought she would of at least wiggled around. I know she didn't just do what I think she did. "You F_cki_g cock sucker!" Then she flicked the wicks on me, landed a middle finger, Umm! And burnt rubber before I even had an opportunity to apologize.

"Say Wreck, I'm kinda booked right now. I'mm hit you in uh' hour. Let me know if it's anything you need me to do."

"Gotcha." The horn hung up. Almost like ta' forgot about "Lady Soljia" sitting in front of me. "What's up with you though?" I quizzed her, but not looking for our convo going into debts. But with no hitting below the belts game poured like heels clocks dough at two thousand and some per lid, you dig! And not once had she raised the bar on getting some loochie, so you know I wasn't pressed. And she was on E.S.P.N time. But the lust in her eyes held more unanswered questions than I prepared for. After taking inventory, my thoughts were on a different level. If you haven't experienced these forms of episodes, keep on living. Which my position for Lady Soljia, it was quite simple. "This the only reason you stopped me simply for the satisfying your curiosity?" She fired back the expected.

"Nah, not in the least bit, but I'm hopeful you enjoyed this opportunity of me flirting with you Mr. Maxwell."

"Is that right? Answer this, has anyone even warned you that uh' women's feet matches her panties?" As the both of us had to laugh that one off. As her response held its own pulse, saying the least.

"No, you're the first. It's awkward you mentioned that because guess what, I've questioned myself along those same lines. Gotta quizz for you too."

"Is dat right, please don't let me be the reasons your tongues tied. Speak what's on your mind love, don't be scared. Gon' do the damn thang!" As I insisted her honesty.

"Well, you leave no other options but putting forth uh' response that's equal, satisfying and justified." I like ta lashed out something I knew I'd had to back track. But I quietly held it in. Plus, it was further than the adventures of Max's lifestyles. I'm used ta' putting smiles upon faces! Without doubt rang different something about her, she was on another type of hype, which sparked like danger. Making a bigger prospect out of cuteness. Likely cause she hadn't tested herself against the full rules of the four levels, maybe too, that's the reasons Uncle fly suggested, I hadn't had the stomach for the other levels the game of life parachutes. Again, that's just Unk, having an unforeseen vision from the ups and downs, bouncing back-n-forth between the varies upon the Jaguarz and the sloths. But not to wrench. Lil mama looks weren't bad, it's just after my encounter with "Delishis Gap" my standards gotten prejudice for any other urges. Yet I do apologize Ladies, but once you know you have a "Mer-vielle" marvelously wonderful women. Aide-toi, leciel t'ai-dera " Help yourself and heaven may help you." it's what I believe the foundation of life present. Whether in   English or French the language doesn't matter. The scope presumes. As Lady Soljia hadn't quit. Submitted, in her protest, She nerves. "Well, I suppose a man's feet oughta match his pockets. No question." And I hinted That's why I'mm keeping a pair of "Air-Day-I-Dream-About-Sunsets (ADIDAS) close and idling, gawk to these heels. Society to flimsy these days, nor am I the dude who desires raggedy kicks. Life's potentials requires thinking outside the box. In the utmost politest way, I motioned Lady Soljia put it in reverse. Had her to revisiting the drawing boards, Still yet, she wasn't ready for the drift.

Taking deep breaths, inhaling the weed leaves which filled the space of my ride. While outta the rear views blindside was O.H.A. (Oakland Housing Authority), aka our neighborhoods project wanna be police. And they be tryin extra hard to extract dudes off the blocks, those looking to put uh' meal on they tables. Most of the times going harder than the real O.P.D (Oakland Police Department).

"This I do not need right now, for these wanna be cops pulling me over and fucking off my high, I just got finished with uh' bid. Plus, dis' my last bit of cookies. Just as I spoke look who appears out of nowhere. The red and blue lights bluripping! I dreaded going on another high speed, which did not work out to well my last

run-ins, my own mama she was unable recognizing

her baby. Those ol' police put hands and cleeks, dig that! Nearly laxed ah' dude, noticeable war wounds. Man my chin almost twice the size of an oversize pumpkin. Which I'm not about to lie, has taught me uh' sure thing-do not second guess or hesitate getting further. No pausing ya' moves, gone proceed. Burn rubber and or pull it over you won't survive doing both. I'm not promoting danger. And it's unlikely you'll rarely outrun the radios, just saying, not in these days in ages.

"breaka, breaka one-two I've gotta male black driving south bound on Havenscourt and Bancroft. In a green'ish, new Lamborghini It has no license plates, which was obvious the officer musta forgot his radio was blasting on intercom. I pulled over to avoid the hassles. The officers quickly drew their services weapons.

"Place your hands on the steering wheel, please." Officer Phoenix ordered me. As I replied, while studying his badge just in case. You knowing how they be on some trigger happy, gotta stay alert round here. "There we go with this ol' shit again. As I glared outta my rear view while admonishing myself, in the same takes keeping my comments of how I felt on the "D-L" (DownLow). Following proper protocols making the right moves.

"Who's car have you ripped off young man?" The officer struck.

"Excuse you!" I rudely answered. Batting uh' thousand with my eyelids, concealing what I wanted and or maybe should had fed.

"Try facing forward, straight ahead, put uh' smile on your face that wouldn't decrease your chances in your favor." As I smirked, but not loud enough getting his attention. Then relaxed with my hands on the wheel, noticing that might help. Sounded the officer.

"While reaching for your identification Mr. Kool Breeze, leave your hands in plan sight." Officer Phoenix barked. The others assisting him they stared, ready to take action, upon any gestures unpermitted.

"Was that suppose to be some kinda insult?" the officer asks. I didn't' intend for it to be, but it darted the wrong way. "Where's your driver license? Cut out the bullshit." I fought from going off the hinges.

"No! what gives you permission for pulling me over?" I felt my comments lit the torch. What did I do that for.

"Hey, Parker, we've got uh' smart alek," yells the other officer, one of the four-piece unit. Two were plainclothes, as their doors slung open, wit' billy clubs brandished ready looking to repeat what kicked off in South Central decades ago causing riots. I wondered, what in the hell they'd needed their whole force for a lousy traffic stop. It'll be different had I made uh' dash or tried resisting, but I didn't as much bip, bop or fart. I held my grounds. My shit checked out in a heart beat, and off I dipped about my daily routine. And no warrants had registered not yet then, from my Parole agent. But I'm now praying nothing shows until I'm at least outta their distance of sight. No sooner than reaching the next intersection instantly, I readjusted my sounds, the woofers were banging folks two and three blocks down the way could have had entertainment. As if I replaced their home stereos. Like being seated right in their living room quarters.

And you heard grannie screaming at the top of her lungs once pulling into the driveway. "Turn that dang on music off, or down, it makes no sense for anyone playing music that dog gon' loud." And most of the time she was right, but you know us ghetto children don't be listen. Freshest Lambo out, only one of the few players in the hood who was leaning on plates like those. As dudes whole personalities have three-sixty'd, but I maintained my focus as I prepared to hit "Daytona Beach," getting ready for the shipping trailer. Expect nothing other, cuzz dats what players do.

Meanwhile, today's an exception relaxation day. Sunday, and I don't wanta be bothered with a soul. Jamming "Sade," Ordinary Love. Got the whole block rockin' out with my favorite parts on repeat. "This isn't no ordinary love, I keep crying for you, I keep." You know how she attaches to a person's inner most parts of the human soul. Yea, exactly.

"That's my joint! The ladies lose their thoughts over her every time. But on the real, I don't be paying much attention, only watching da' eyes. Going "damn! He's looking like he's booked, spoken for." Yet despite; they'll dip on out there anyhows. "Us men, we frankly be's no help. But, ladies, what's with you, not holding that widespread. Be's just testing our Integrity, character, and moral standards, without letting go!" Then quick to forfeit. These days I'm just saying though, dudes we be needing uh' lil better communications- and I'mm leave that whereas at, outta the way for now. First gotta quick question, Is it impossible denying the likes of an "Ayesha Diaz." "No, most certainly not! Do I disagree the assumptions, the glitters ain't always gold. "Probably not. There's gotta be room for exceptions, Like the "Lambo" gift. Oooch! But anyhows, us dudes gotta be sharper on our toes, on our "A-1-game." Otherwise we'll endure the heartaches and marginal breaks, not to ignore the way Lambo's coming more than just one formats these days. And know I'm "forever jealous of my realness." As there's those whom altogether traded their shields for the latest Prada Sandals, and how might we forget those Vicky famous Aimis thongs. Nowadays, notches they standing across the streets utilizing a different gauge- with a hypocritical finger aimed, letting it be known "rightfully" It's gon' cost a mighty fortune to obtain their unconditional love, which I'm not opposed of, but some cry foul cause our intentions are often misunderstood, yet, may reshape our next Malcolm X's, or could become our today's Barak Obama. Yet it's often underscored and in exchange for something priceless. Let me stop. I know I'm Jawsn, but not draining the wells. You knowing! And I'm paying attention. As inferences are a mutha, but why censor our thoughts. Which often end up caught under murky provisions. I'd prefer pushing up and tackle battles in unisons, It's the best option for neutralization for change over periods of time. But still It appears a never ending quest. Yeah there's gonna be ups-N-downs, growth, developments on the roads to achieving victory's. But a thousand miles begins with a single step, starting and not stopping. Heaven requires this of us."

Women known to be psychic
and heard to read minds.

CHAPTER

8

Immediately as I bounce through the front door of Granny's, it was on like chicken over waffles. "What's done happen-now-with-you-child! Your parole officer is looking for you. They've been to the house, your auntie Olive's and your mother's place. You know, I hope it's not about that new car you just purchased. Where'd you get it from?" Grams had no idea about the wreck as I hadn't let anybody know. Thinking it'll go unnoticed. But in the back of my mind I knew my license plates were subjected to becoming revealed to the officials. They've got those street cams now on just about every cross intersection which it's uh' good thang, depends which side of the yard stick you're positioned. Although, I hadn't violated any rules, but lets not forget still, I'm a parolee leaving the scene with "Delishis" which wasn't criminal misconducts, not that I'm aware of. It wasn't no hit and run, oops! I forgot about the surprise visit we shared. But two adults consensual fore play isn't skid-row material. It's America, aren't you innocent until proven guilty, at least those are the assumptions of mines. But lets not get ahead of the game, which maybe she'll vouch for who was in the right if I have to ever answer, I suppose. While looking for breathing room I asked Grannie, had my agent inquired about me having anything to do with wrecking my Porsche? She responded No. Although, it was on the noon news, at least my Photograph was. G'moms was historical warning. "Your parole officer didn't mention anything about the reasons for his per say visit. "Did anybody get hurt?" Grams meddled. "Not that I'm aware of." She ensured, " Ho-ney you betta be careful, driving so fast." "OK, gotcha Grams!" As I baited still finding it non negotiable to muster how I might be getting put on trial for a dingy wreck. How? Without an official known victim's Idenity. A reportedly bystander dialed 911, supplying my license plate number which insisting the subject driving the Porsche departed the scene with one of the hurt victims, as the others took off running on foot. They provided a vague description of the driver the days following the incident. As it improvised was vary scares.

"A young male, black very youthful, wearing dark clothing, gloves, a head garment, with facial full beard. He disappeared so quickly his full identifying features could not had been gathered. "But six months later now I'm looking at the Bay Area News and a photograph of guess who pops up? bulletin depicts.

"Bay Area Oakland man's on the loose for the vehicle wreck near Piedmont and Broadway on Thanksgiving Day. Leaves several victims in serious but stable condition. Bystanders in proximity to the wreck, stated the African American suspect was in his mid-twenties who was driving the black "Cayan Porsche" ran into the Lexus GS 400 traveling at a speed over the limits. But was obviously able to exit his vehicle and assisted the hurt victims of the other vehicle involved. One of the apparent victims departed the scene uncertain whether in the "SUV" or not it's unclear, but both are still of large." "Maxwell Pixar." He's reportedly the driver. Police has identified him as owning the utility vehicle, and residing in the Oakland area.

Took no time for the news to spread like uh' wild trail blaze throughout the town. It went global yesterday! On net speed. While no one had any clues for the reasoning. But there's this widely range of public "frenzy." Folks from the States Capital, down to Washington D.C. are committing on this Thanksgiving Day wreck on Piedmont Boulvard involving some guy whose reportedly uh' felon. They've revealed his identity as "Maxwell Pixar." Interesting how the facts of him being wanted appears to be controlling any substance of the dialogue that's out there. Still it's kinda cloudy for whatever reasons. But "strikingly" as I overhead these two elder women engaged with conversations riding the back of public's local transportation debating. I myself, happened to be pushing enroute downtown Oakland headed hopping onto a Greyhound Bus to get outta state to Texas to visit family. Just letting the dust settle before dipping out again into the forefronts. And I'm getting spotted "off the rip." Hell, I Couldn't leave offa' my porch until somebody was knockin' at me, "Shining with da' lights out." Think not! Try getting a surprise knock on your front door, for any type of warrant. Simplest as, getting uh'

J-walking incident. People's dialogues becomes utterly unsurrell. Just try stopping by your homies tilt after you're wanted and see their initial responses. "It's what you about to do, I have to take the kids to a medical visit, or I'm on my way to work, you know it's getting late the kids gotta be up at seven in da' morning fa' school. Not sabotaging anybody in particular, but our friends and some family too are amazing. Be prepared for the dry wits. It's more drama on those fields than running a play in the bottom the fourth quarter, down uh' field goal, with half the distance of the goal to travel.. And in humid heat, and it's the super bowl, seconds on the clock and it's ticking. I do acknowledge there's rules for applying half time type of blinders, requiring you to focus. But that Azz be's on those hips of performers and cheerleaders, you talking about parking lot party starters needs no further references, from the Bay to MIA.

Makin' my rounds back safely home to Omega's, lil mama had the parking lot barking like a soul food kitchen was burning. Right what I needed, after inhaling that sticky lime greenery eating away at the few active brain cells lingering still barely intact. At the front door she greets her babe landing the biggest wettest kiss. In one hand lived ah' 16 ounce glass of cold water, indeed needed. The other baked chicken wings, mustard greens, yams and my favorite fried rice. Um! Knowing whenever she cooks, her foots in the dish, I'm just placing notice. And at times, it's not without signaling, "one or the other." She wants either the latest Givenchy threads and purses. And best be prepared for the after show her looking forward to her "Proper-ish" if you know how ghetto women rock. And she deserved that! No question, with a meal prepared as this was, I couldn't go wrong, regardless how whichever the dice landed. My vote was voluntary. Reasons you never trust the wabbles with big butts and juicy smiles. Anything's liable. Pimps the best of us every time. Surely wouldn't you disagree! Yeah, right. She understood and knew my reasoning. "Always catching me off guard with my hand in my pockets. It's like giving food to a tank of hungry piranhas. Best assure, they'll dip to the rise every time for uh' bit. "Unless" they're fed and nourished properly." As they should, yup!

"So babe, what's owed for such hands down thoughtful moments you've just delivered this evening?" Her soft-spoken response didn't help the situation, had me cautious.

"You know I measured my ingredients in hopes of

matching your taste buds." Even without fully grasping what she was getting at, I proudly advanced my options. "My offers uh' "P.B.I." I Prancly danced out there for Omega's approval. But she looked bravely, if insulted, what's your flavor? "Hon' I haven't the slightest idea of what in the hell uh' P.B.I`s about. But okay. Sounds good, let me know soonest you ready." Just the way it filtered offa her lips had a conversation of dread coupled with expectations that had to be kept. I fought easing the load by suggesting, "Don't worry, I'm certain you'll do well." Omega paraded in her most confident stare. "Whatever." But you'd better not leave without ensuring a smile, Or you won't be getting seconds! This inference larked but didn't afraid me nor had I deterred. As I licked out my tongue humbly. "Forty-nine, let me owe you the other one." Winking letting her know the rebounds looked mighty plushed, If she decided alone those routes. Her response;

"Quit playing cause you know I'm born ready to make you bring just dat!" Then I peered upwards, Omega strutted off half-naked, while dressed in almost near to nothing. I stopped her between strides, insisting.

"To answer your question uh' "P.B.I." means. Then I caught myself. That's aliight, I'mm show you better-what I meant." She went like, "Wooh, I guess you can learn something new every day." You know it! Just as surest you keep yo' eyes on the prize. She replied in her nonchalant body language which spelled, "You too much for T.V. love." "And I suppose we both share the same vision." Like you wouldn't know. My insinuations fired right back. Thinking deeply absent responses. This is one evening she has me ready to drink shots of cognac outta the arch of her back. "Boy, these fried wings tasted like shrimp. I couldn't graphs why we were not taking orders out online for the sales." As I encouraged, but didn't get far.

"No, I don't think so.. plus you wouldn't know how to ack any hows." Omega styled.

"You know finger licking comes natural, anything concerning you." I couldn't help but reply while dearly invested in her next response. "Why is dat!" Omega snapped, then batted, which almost led me second questioning myself. Yet knowing the answer. I guess just to untangle what else slick might fumbled outta her pearly whites. And she never fails. "Because when I'm baking for you, it's my heart and soul, and sometimes I go far as dippin a titty or two in the batter givin' it that needed tasty ghetto flavor. Which you take for granted quit oftenly, I must say."

"No, fo' real though, I ought know how we ain't opening up shop on these banging recipes you be bringing to the table." Before going further I panned myself.

"Okay, I could muster the wings exclusively but the other side dishes, let's consider us makin' uh' few, two's and fews."

These thoughts alone dripped money signs threw my mind. It's times my non-stop thinking ideas of placing her wings and sauce on da' market weren't far-fetched, for the right price. But I dared to speak of such braveness. I'm sure it wouldn't been to difficult. As tasty as her fingers were, no disputes. They're absolute party starters. Let me stop before she catch uh' whiff of what I'm cooking up. Cause you know women, known to be psychic, and herd to read minds. Knowing Omega she'd raise the roof probably set my clothes outside, had I positioned my thoughts to even gestured, any inkling of the thoughts. She gazed back while floating by with dat lil rubber band waistline, biting outta' this world, OMG! and cutting her eyelids like she knew something I didn't know, unmeasured plays in mind? I kinda teased.

"What's wrong with you?" She was perking and surfing. I lied, responding. "Nothing. just admiring." Dang! Why am I frost bitten, stuck in a daze. As the sound waves of Anita Baker, "Sweet Dreams" took me sailing. Omega sang along, making the evening that much more bubbly. Brought out about my piece of mind equivalent sitting quietly and at peace by the Orient Beach site. How she frisked underneath delivered via the slippery worded phrases, had the effects of releasing a throbbing sensation. Relaxing the nerve vessels reaching beyond, into a deep outer layer which it's known evident registers with satellites. The notions of the "P.B.I." which was about to be soon undreamth. "But in the purest form."

As I opted phonological processing her body in mind, from head to toe, letting her beauty breathe on, without loosing a drip. As I prayed for this opportunity to become our nonce reality, and not just a dream she'd renege exploring. Once the lights were dimmed, radiance of lust was fully beneath the surface and at attention. I prepared for the hourglass to enjoy the results of the evening smooth listings of "K.B.L.X." That's (The Bay Area's number one Jazz station) tucked under the sun like two invisible soulmates. Light thunder showers, pushed up against the windowpanes, causing our moods to speak in hush tones. The only disturbance rendered was from noises my pager made adjacent my belt buckle over off to the side in da' corner minding its own business like crazy. As I repress those thoughts even to this day, brings out moments and laughter of our never ending conquest with plenty love still to be shared.

Everything do not always require an answers.

CHAPTER

9

Awaken mid-morning tossing and gruntin' as my heart knew something wasn't right. But I couldn't put a finger what was inching under my soul. I didn't bother getting outta bed. Omega and I we slept the day away. My pager sat beeping stashed in between the couch. It was there at my discretions. Now holds lingering questions for answers. But it just wouldn't quit beeping. I knew it had to been of importance, by the number times between the beeps. Upon I retrieved the device and noticing the numbers, in disbelief majority were followed by code 911. Which almost means, more so than likely something unusual, I fussed. The first number I dialed was Grannies house. No answer. That's untypical. I pressed within. Where in the world could she be at this hour. Well, I knew it wasn't like her to not answer her horn at 6:ish a.m. momma's always near posted our home fronts during those hours with her Hometown's cup of coffee with one foot on the stove tuned in, looking over her next racetrack bet. Ready to summon Miss. Maggie her best friend who places her bets to the fields. These were Granny's rituals of her daily parlay. Besides she always gotta kick outta and loved to be the first to deliver and receive the neighborhoods gossip. Which is funny cause her and my Auntie "Lori" has what appears to be a friendly contest of who know the beans first. They be parading back and forth loud in laughter's unlikes anything you've seen these days. There's families doing just the opposites, "What in the world in God's living ways our society has resulted to." I have the slightest idea, but it's not gone bother what im doing. Have any solutions? I'm praying. I haven't quite believing in the brighter days ahead.

As I dialed the second numbers on my pager a receptionist answered.

"Highland General Hospital. How may I be of assistance to you?" I instantly felt a sharp pain in my chest, followed with a hollow twist, still yearning to be fulfilled as my initial gut thoughts were what's don' happen now. The gates of precisions floated. The state of losing any sibilant it holds no place on earth. That's when I discovered one of my closest pals just up and departed us from reckless gun play. The bullets tore off one of his legs, the others punctured his lungs. Tears begun pouring like puddles of storms. I went to the floor like uh' brand new Ferrari Sports Coup on four flat tires and couldn't move for what appeared like weeks. The burden was weighing me down as if someone had poured concrete into my shoes. My world stopped! I lost the homey "X.R" they say he ran from the neighborhood decoys, and they gunned him down in broad lit daylight. No weapon was found at the scene. Although it's reportly he aimed something looked like uh' shiny object, but you know how those things gets, we've seen and heard that flick uh' million times. "X.R" wasn't only a homey but was more of ah' brother type. We grew up and through up hustling together. Whatever I didn't have and it was within distance of his, I didn't have to raise uh' finger nor ask, and vice versa. That's how we rocked! The feelings were as if an entire world rested upon my shoulders alone and sound. For the first time ever Omega seen me torn apart in a state of denial. Teardrops had poured like uh' Marquett King, kicking three's. "Babe, what's wrong?" As I wanted badly answering, but the frog stuck in my throat had won on that battle. Only thing my body was abled to do was motions of the head, in grief. In a state of hopelessness, followed by silence. There wasn't anything anybody could offer to replace the void. Me and "X.R." were niched like gravel without a planet, non-existent. Wherever you seen him, look, I'm posted right there- as always likewise. Devastated by this tragic loss, my mind it just snapped! No one uh' never comprehend, our hard fought struggles. Through the hood trenches, as I grabbed my belongings and headed out the front door, Omega she tried to stop me, but was paused like an unfinished sentence. Waiting still to this day to be completed. As there's obviously things a person goes through in life which doesn't always require an answer, it's enough from the visuals that appears through others facial expressions, as most of my days progressing were spent quietly in deep thought, solitary had lent it's best friend. I detached from others whose forms conflicted with decisions chosen opposite of mines. Although, the support of Omega's and my bound kinda' never quite rebounded the same following the Thanksgiving collision. We still continued and became the best business partners outright and life hasn't looked more promising.

A book still incomplete whereas it's absent it's authentic purpose.

CHAPTER

10

For the love of more than just money. Today that resonates, it doesn't linger with detours. Omega and I begun our lifes planning's, just withing seconds, It was just yesterday we were on the brightest roads, but it's no love lost, just we share two different realities in worlds unintentional non-restraint from one another. I frown having misplaced our experiences by no defaults of hers. Thinking every women supposed to shape their better other half, that's yearned for, but in life those options aren't necessarily guaranteed. You work for having those availabilities, absent effort there's not foreseeable journeys. Our vision had dimmed, but I'm forever grateful of the lessons along the way. As our bounds the two of us kept in tack, maintaining at the headquarters we facilitated our marketing and merchandising for "Vogue Tires Entertainment." Bro, Network, France and myself have rebounded over these past few weeks. We've yet discussed in depths about the homey we lost "X.R." Perhaps not that I'm inferring anything surrounding his absence, didn't have anything on the agenda particularly. I decided to ring up "France" and gather his inputs for our up and coming scheduled trip next month. Daytona Beach in Florida, it's about to be off da' charts! I dialed his horn.

"You heard what's popping down in Miami next month bro?"

"Naw, what it do?" France responded itching to learn.

"Daytona on the beach." As I answered tryna' act like I knew more than I'd known on my in`s and outs. But for real, I just learned hours ago having overheard these two sistas talking about how they wasn't abled to wait, getting down South to meet one of those looted out country boys. I'm like, you ain't gotta travel that far lil moma, I'm just touching down outta' Texas and my pockets coincide. You know how they be rocking out yanda! But I didn't rub it in. Just reflected and kept on pushing about my peaceful day, while brushing at my natural Ocean waves. Yet, not misjudging the grass thinking it's greener on the other side, being extra careful. Guess who Chic was doing majority of the Jawsn?"

"Who?" France quickly snapped looking surprised, like she couldn't been on his interest list. I heard that! Still though I only incented. And stayed outta getting to deep in on it.

"Don't say nothing to anybody, cause bad news travels and considerably in this little-bity ass city." France browsed as if I'd lost my mind before responding. "That's who dipping in and outta lanes, fess up. Quit playing bring the noise."

"And you bet not put it on to thick. But Network and the homey D.J, swears it's yo' lil thang "Angelica Storm" outta Hayward who was yapping da' most about dipping out there with a crew planning on working they ol' slipper game, her and her pontes from Cal. State Hayward."

"Ri-ght, yeaaah, that's big! I've been on her heels thick for a minute hoping she would land me uh' presidential, she be doing her hey-lo thizzal- wit dat Azz on her, um! She just banged for a Platinum Joint Network was rocking with those Ricky Rossay cough drops, flooded with marble size diamonds. You peep dat shit? The wrist and bezel – no Jawsn though, lil mama cain't stay up offa' my line, tryna get me to invest. And I'm damn sho debatin putting like uh' half of Thanksgiving in the bank on the gouch, over the weekend. But you gotta push Monday morning before they round off the stacks, that's that you know old "O.T" work, but I fooled around and fumbled and uh' player from Delaware got on her bumpers and got the rebounds. I'm pissed, but on my shit though brah! I ain't heard or seen nothing outta her since. Last I gotta dose on her she was in Foot Locker with uh' "L-7" on a splurging full spree buying dude the latest high end sports apparel gear. Those "NBA" M.J's, big boy kicks the two bands uh' better type. You know, I almost braked but I didn't lean on her. I overheard Uncle Fly cautioning me.

"Youngsta' never come between uh' soul getting they loochie." That's real drill. As I bounced outta' my own way uh' few steps.. while leaving her proper room ta' groom doing stock moves, players do.

"You shoulda' kept lil mama on deck" France whisked and parted out. Yeah, I'm hipped shit happens but I'm not the dude ta' be crying over spilled milk. She knew the score, plus how to utilize those hips, fingers and heel-strikers mightily swell. That being said I quickly grabbed my car keys and beckon upon France; we'll get together in the "thirty-third," meaning the days ahead. Before dipping making rounds around the city it was almost about time school was letting out and ain't nothing like a tender eye hawking the gold shoes on tonka toys whips. I'm leaning, growling music barking, zapco board in the red zones, which signified my woofers fifteen inch "E.V.E.'s" were doing they *thugg thizzal'* but uh' tad bit to loud, otherwise the board lights wouldn't been in the red zone cabbage patch dancing, busting uh' move.

"Bro, get at your parole agent and see if you're

abled to get a leave for next month to slide to Daytona Beach in Florida." Gazing, France's reactions he wasn't looking the least enthused about venturing out, but it wasn't enough for causing me to rearrange what I'd been planning since last years. Which was way over limitations, and this Year's not looking to let up. It's flooded with promotions on a grand scale. Flyers, posters and internet posting everywhere and you know how college women rockz. "Off the hook nonstops." Connecting in flocks and some beyond worth betting on. You'd invite home to the Ohana, that's Hawaiian for family. Imagine dat!

The next Sunrise you know I couldn't keep still from dashing for the Benzo dealership for the past few weeks. I've had my sight on pulling up in that black on black S500 Mercedes. Fits uh' young dude spectacular as if none other. But some of the homies out the Bay 707 Area spent through the block back to back upping the ante and they riding the S600's, but the price sticker tag on those windshields be yelling "Police about to be everywhere." But who gives ah' damn, it's summer and my time to floss and anyhows, it's not my fault uh' young entrepreneurs gifted and only twenty-one years his youth. Living life to the fullest with enough gawp to exercise his max hand off the lot, spanking brand new, paid in full. It was only two at the time on the dealer's floor, and you know those assholes had the audacity to look twice at me like as if money in the ghetto's differs from the kind capable pushing one of those off their floors. Like excuse you! Now I'm here posted for assistance going on what appeared almost maybe, an half an hour, which might be putting extras not there, but dice off about half dat, aliiht! But, I'm front and center showroom floor. And not a salesperson approaches to ask if I wanted a test drive or interested in making a purchase. Loot ready to be spent, and no, I hadn't come in there brown paper bag danglin. Like probably most my peers woulda. I moved with a more business prospect intent, tryna to be conservative at least that's what my contentions were. Stopped at the bank, "Wells Fargo, for a directly withdrawal deposits, information was verified, and even the teller had beef. Looking at me way-of-outta pocket and hinted.

"You know the I.R.S. about to be knocking with major questions." I almost said. Fuck it. But if you work for yours, you make big boys noise, with big boys toys. Yeah, whips included. If someone has an issue with dat. Then at the end of the day, it's not your fault. They should just do better next round, cause flossing is the way. And you might just oughta hang on to those receipts fo' glue. "Collectively" I've begun to visual actions more seriously now than ever, while exploring the stacks. Placing notices for brighter commitments, at the same dance expanding on my marginal merits, thinking outside the box.

The floor man approaches me, not looking bitter, It's like bet! Casual behavior, I'm chilling not to mention he was the only person who appeared to have had any sense to recognize game had it stared him in his lids. "Sir, you'll look magnificent sliding outta here hugging corners under the wheels that black on black S500. Those are considered "Big Boys Toys." I ought see why not. I looked with a grin matching my pockets, but didn't wanta scare the dude off.

"How would you be financing that today?' He spoke like he was ready for his commission forthwith, in cash. However. Fives, tens, twenties, fifties, didn't matter longest it added up. It was fine on his watch. And he wasn't interested in the I.R.S, A.D.S. or anybody else. His duty was putting food on his table at home and making happy customers, my kinda language.

He reached his hand out to sweaty prints. Before introducing myself, I wiped my hands on my shirt, then offered my fingertips, the hoods "no prints dapper." Then introduced myself.

"Maxwell Pixar"

"Nice to meet you."

" I'm from the other side of the bridge Oakland. I'm interested in that S500 Black."

"My pleasure, Jihan Belair thanks for choosing our dealership. He phrased.

"You made a golden choice." Excited woulda been

an understated suggestion. I didn't trip. Why? Shit it was only minutes until painting da' town black, sun'up ta' downs.

"Thank you sir"

"Bet, I'll be paying cash." I reached into my shirts pocket and Placed a verified wire transfer slip in his hands, already signed, and transferred with our both banking and routing numbers, which was obtained the day before. Uh' hundred and nineteen racks.

"Wooh, you're quick on the draw." You musta' had your mind made up some time ago. Have you driven the S500 before?"

This he quizzed outta his pitch.

"Not yet, but I'm prepared for the roads ahead. If you have any extras over the amount you're welcome. Keep dat!"

Without losing site of the steering wheel. That's when I offered. "I like personalized license plates and those to read as "Beyond," That's B-E-Y-O-N-D. You know how folks get when money at they tables. Amped up. And he wasn't anything different. Eyes lit up like Independence Day. I just looked and shook my head, but on the inside, you know my Ste-Lo. But I didn't valve as much. Withheld my smile. Which one couldn't imagined what it vetted. "Let those co-workers of yours know never judge books by its covers looks hold intuitions and known to be unforgotten."

"Right."

"You could say that again." As Belair replied, which fueled his consensual gestures. If I might unsolicited, wasn't anything other than authenticity about his equality services provided from start to finish. Furthermore, who cared if I wasn't dressed in a Hugo Boss three-piece suit and tie hugging me like I just ripped peeled out on somebody, and shoes laced up tight like skates. But one thing for sure you cannot argue at "It's Money." It's nondiscriminatory. And that's what I love about it. After selling a hundred thousand independently musical CD's outta the trunk of my latest release on Vouge Tires Ent. Who gave uh' damn, who inquired about the Freshest Kidd on the block. Shit at six bucks uh' unit. That's not including any show money nor paraphernalia merchandise. Trust it doesn't take a rocket scientist to configure what my margin was looking like. That's just one release. Never would it be of need to apologize. That's just the ghetto about me. Didn't mean to rub that in like grease, but I'm here to represent hood money. It spends. And I'm just as hood as surest my names "Maxwell Pixar." Before even finishing at the dealership I'm valuing dudes hating a player. And I haven't even danced through the blocks. Not to underscore, those sales folks who be smiling in yo' face at the same time back biting, like wishing the

"I.R.S" pulls up and shut it down on a Chefs. Not only was it brought out right, but I politely let it be known that I came predetermined on leaving fully serenaded. That's despite any scrutiny. When my time arrived to test drive things got real kosher, but I withheld my desires and precisely declined.

"No thank you, but if something goes wrong within five years, fifty thousand miles, you'll be the first to know. I'm in a hurry, with plenty lasagna on my plate." Revealing my most prestigious looks, while pouring over the factory warranty forms. As I began to notice the shock-waves from the other assistants, puzzled like damn! I shoulda, coulda, been first to sense that big catch. "Belair" earned himself every bit of an extra $4,500 just on what my differences were off the price tag. Not including his in house pay. Soonest I departed the road, I knew I became the star-burst of ignorance, being that I hadn't even test drove the vehicle and spent uh' hefty near two-hundred thousand. But it's what you pose of the reputation of a brand new S500 Benzo-rel, I needed not to question it's performances. My attention stayed tuned into my Nakamichi sounds blasting out the sunroof top- the best of the D.O.C formula you couldn't said anything to me to ruin my day. Wouldn't been of any relevance had you sought. The very first person I notified was "France." Alerting him of the good news, although I fought resisting given him info knowing he'd made the whole posse aware. As I believed I'd hustled and by choice earned first bragging rights.

And boy, didn't not or not I'd made properly usage of my options. Talking about flossing, I bumped the bars up four notches. And my stocks under those same realms.

I blurp Frances' cell phone to get a reading whether not he'd heard if his parole officer wasn't opposed of him skiddin' out.

"France what's up, you heard anything yet about the trip? It's around the way-ways. Booking up quickly, rooms and traveling?"

"Brah, dude's whole roster looking to get potential outta town leaves for that Daytona on the Beach events." France pushed.

"Yeah, but did he say it was G-14 fourteen classified?" (meaning its official). "Mann, he's on some bullshit. But I'mm hit da' horn around near three'ish P.M to see what's what. I don't believe there's any reasons in particular for him to deny the request. I haven't had any dirty urine samples within six months." I made an objection rightfully placed.

"Look, say you have a business venture out there. I'll vouch for you since you know "Vouge Tires Ent." On the radars. That's better than a visit for uh' love adventure plus, anything to do with music nowadays, they are hawking twice at thinking it's drug or gang related, with violence attached to it. Which is only a practical forefront to undermine any intended set of intentions preventing our youthful crowd from exploring having a good time." That in itself I found was kinda disturbing. Society we oughta appreciate the friendly activities not to differentiate, but there shouldn't be barriers up, where blinders are better suited. Wouldn't you not agree? That's only an opinion. Inferences, but sadly making relevance doesn't often translate or ship any momentums, not always. Most of the times it requires actions and steadily paced. Even still the results are unwritten, although after several tearful incidents within our communities it's placed our hip-hop scene on over neighborhood watches. Yeah, we can only blame ourselves cause we're so vicious in the kitchen, but I'm mindful of our sentries, "calculators," as our deterrence would not make any reasonable logics. Yet, there's a difference between going too hard in the paint versus handling your fax. Let there be something in our favor we'll pretend it's not there, won't rectify until it's to late up against the zenith's wire wheels burning rubber. I argue, let's impose with camaraderie, having a burst of self-discipline and enjoy prominence for becoming inspired, why not everybody just be open minded opt level playing fields for enabling us to achieve our fair shares. Isn't that what our civil rights fight was hinged based on during the 1960s Revolutionary investments, but I acknowledge grievously hasn't much changed as there's individuals even today still unprepared to stomach another person getting paid legit. Get over it. Discounting one's own creative swag in order to satisfy fetching an hypothesis with an inconclusive goal. There's notta' range to solve the underly, the book still is incomplete whereas it's absent it's real purpose. And the hip hop scene yes, has evolved and now supply inroads for the urban "society," Thankfully our hoods clubhouses has risen to a level of brotherhoods, now we're striding global wise. Yet, even still it's raising eyebrows of questionable activities that surrounds it's territories. But in what world of business there hasn't been ups-n-down sizes, to be vigorously frank. The respect level for entertainment wouldn't be displaced not saying that is what our debates about, had we reevaluated it's perspectives and assumptions to match it's designed romance, as it's multi-billions involved. Thus, unity is required. But only in numbers and maintaining and holding those stances will we get to see results in widely spread vice-grips. We used to hold court in the streets, that's half of what's of topic, which comes with a share of innocent lost with scrapes and bruises. It's fact not fiction, as I'm learning the best teachers are from "errors" acknowledged.

"If you want it, fight for it and hustle with it." Our hands grand, that's how we living outside.

If it's yours for keeps it'll speak for itself.

CHAPTER

11

Beauty they say is hard to tame, ain't that the truth. I'm minding my own, clubbing at "The Twilight Zone" one of our well-know flockin' clubbing spots in the Bay Area, mainly for dudes having exquisite bild folds. Popping bottles and hawking models, just stirring it up maxin. Try being on the dance floor under uh' six with a floor packed with nothing other than dimes topflight beauty queens. You'll catch da' business so rapidly. Matter fact, I doubt seriously if the bouncer letting you pass go. When I quote "off the Whips" this joints fully equipped with nothing other than lifestyles of bling bling's, owned by the Bay Areas "Brian Shaw" and the "Kidd" himself Jason Kid. Few of the town's top elites N.B.A's highly most respected known to handled the rock, that's on and off the lacquer, no need to front. I'm at opened bars, poppin it you know doing "Maxwell Pixar" flirting with one of the finest bartenders with uh' wad in mitts. This lil fine sexy Azz almond pice danced through. Well dipped profounded, hips and everything was in the right places, and I'm not advertising nor high capping, just doing what money does. Appreciating the random bites of the finest things life has to offer humankind.

Quietly fetching from a distance, "Come here with yo' lil thick Azz." I motioned my two inner fingers to get her undivided attention, music was bouncing off the ground, felt as if there was an earthquake. Still it's obvious lil mama had to notice.

"Yeah, you! Say, you mind us sharing uh' bottle that Moet hon, it's on me?" Yeah, I know she heard me! As I thought how she gazed over my direction. When she dialed back, it's as if she'd musta dropped something. Before responding it's how she peered. "I'm sorry but sweety, I have to pour it out the bottles love, you're not permitted for handling these bottles inside the Twilight Zone. They don't let us give these out." I assumed she hadn't noticed the drawl, but I contended.

"I ain't trippin', whatever it cost, make that happen." I meant slightly more, but didn't go there to avoid the feedback from the reckless eye hawkers. Then I peeled off a stack of the new hundnt's without even counting – right in front of her face and pitched. "You have the Black Labels? Further, you may keep da' change hon." Letting her know I'mm a boss, I don't gotta skirt paying for what I like. She appeared as if I wanted running out on the tab without paying. Just uh' babysitting the bottles, but I'm not into holding hands, hashing bands. I'm leaning focused beyond the waitress sights anyhows on what caught ahold of my attention to begun. This bowlegged super bad something was deserving of the next front cover of "Show Draya" looking every bit of the features of the rarest spread I've ever yet seen. Her body was immaculate. She respectfully tucked away the gifts and quickly pranced over and had the bottles in hand, I flirted to her.

"One's for me, the other, give to the young lady right across the room, directly from us." The waitress smiled, and lead.

"Thank you for the generous tip." As it was. Before sliding out, I noticed her bite was lion tight, anytime she happen strolling by you'd sworn lil mama stole uh' piece of the sky. And her bravery it hadn't hurted her appearances one bit. "You have to know, you're handsome, and I'm unspoken for," she winked. And I hinted with a smile, had her biting. "I'mm keep my eyes on you, here's my business card," which read "*Moet-n Trust-*." Frisking the hell outta my eye lids. Like damn! You shoulda' had somebody photographed her teaser feed, as I pinched myself. Boy, was lil mama stacked! Then she reached into her bra, placing the exact wad of the new faces that I'd given her for the bottles. Just as neatly handed her, she unleashed a genie stare that I doubt even Hallie Berry couldn't recreate had it depended on her next global nominee awards. You'd had to seen my reactions to fully digest the effects. Opened for exploring the arrival of some place new! Those vary instance- held the hoist of my imageries of, "Friends way more important than money." As I froze up for the first time a proposition as hers, had stunned and rotated my next of moves without doubts the four levels the game symbolizes tided in. The list of precautions you study in maintaining how not to screw upon opposition. But, she wasn't anything like worth risking. I knew my diamonds well. If I fumbled this rock kiss da' chase goodbye. This wasn't something learned nor taught how if placed against a stale mate, which maneuver kneels, opposite the other, in order to score that ticklish whale. Do you fish or wiggle back the bait. No, I offer, just study and observe, while positioning and have faith. If it's yours for keeps, it'll speak for itself. But, it does require you to surrender and pay fully attention to the signs. And "Moet" she was lasered in, stayed the direct course- wasn't distracted, which is what I admired about her. She continued getting off her bottles throughout the V.I.P, what I expected of a thoroughbred was pose to do. Unlike the young tender I forwarded the bottle. She was offa' her square for some unknown reasons. Was unfriendly engaged with exchanging dialogue with a dude politicking his rapper's Plato, simply because ol'boy having placed a couple of musical disc on the shelves, I gathered. But from the first looks of impressions homey was being baked. She was frying his lamb chops – dry cooking at that. As you do the famous blow up, ready for sale. As I offered her the bottle believing it would calm her down, and try stopping playboy from slapping the taste buds outta her mouth. Cause ol' dude was in his feelings, but getting a dose of his own medicine. Nothing like ghetto drama. In my opinion he was the one outta pocket. But it was none of my forte. That's how stranger things happen. "For real dough." Had to quiz myself. But stayed dialed, willing-itching a response of hers. As they hashed out in verbal abusive sparring, as it followed.

"I take it you like what's about you?" was not that a lousy punch line of gift of gab. Thinking to myself I know homey coulda' done better with mustering something. I fought not to jab, after how she just tap danced! Woooh! Only in the ghetto. Lil mama, swelly assassinated his character stating."In fact, I find you very unattractive. Those things you glorify sweetheart, the gold chains flooded out watches. But I'm sorry it doesn't ring my bells. Which quit honestly, It's outdated with today's reality. That's what's got our worlds upside down and off balance right now. Where's your drive aimed?" If not for yourself, at least for the ladies that do uphold and maintain some forms of decency and integrity. It's uh' few of us whom still exist. Her verbal's were tumbling smoothly outta her grill like southern home syrup. As I couldn't help but to revisit the unrewarding lifestyles that I once was married to. Home-chick was introducing a side of life, the grown folks edition that I'd grown use to, homey wasn't ready for. But if that was anybody else, likely she'd probably found herself picking up thirty-six dentures off the gravel. The fire in her eyes coulda' lit an Olympics game torch. But the lighter side of him peeked. And he shelved his pride and thank God! That's rarely seen or portrayed how today's youth are. But that's even subjectable to one's opinion. "Go ahead, suit yourself. I'm inflated off public's entertainments absent stand up residuals." But I have to offer he's a much better player than those around our way. And thankfully dude wasn't uh' hater. And respectfully departed without a negative drawl. But something. Just didn't sit well. I questioned. No doubt in my mind. Situations as those, you do the score keeping. I knew he was just about to fry and eat her as a golden lobster side dish. You'd think, but then who wouldn't been upset. Lil mama, "heads bowed," took Twilight Zone by rage. And mind you, those women there will boo you like the Apollo, right up off the stage. Her inferences were valid. But respect goes both ways. It took a helluva dude to dissect his faults, and maybe he had. Although, I won't define. That's his or her's obligations. Good for him humbling himself in order to better obtain the unseen, looking further down the roads. That's what's up. "Next round was my suggestions, then not now. Maxwell! Hush up. Knowing she was raising utilitarian's in hindsight. As I laughed to myself but rethought from the distance her features oughta qualified her as a potential runway. Head to toe she was a through gift unwrapped to be seen at least she prowled, stood further than the zone. Her initial appetite then served only as an appetizer. But

I would be lying if I protested I wasn't full. I learnth ah' thang or two how to honor and analyze life's equations, the notions when to hold in thoughts, versus maybe speaking out in context- factoring in well-proportions hips working overtime, with goals predestined. And those at times, leads to split pea decisions. Which often forces a person acting some other type of ways got you looking for gifts. "You should know!"

Having a platonic state of mind, it's a biology of the four levels glare. One cain't buy that. Tasteful, but grounded, as the "Art of Juicy" but it's not up to me. Just thinking out loud. Instead of going full court press. Yeah, right! So the dude seated besides us, get better positioned and capitalizes on the bottle sent to her table. That's highly unlikely. It's the kinda shit don't fit, but I ought trip. And plus, no sweat, I'm at my best underneath the designer looks fetched any hows. No pressure, and this was perfect, in idea for the life which depending on the freestyle. Without wasting much or any time. I founded upon myself making large steps towards her direction. The Vee-Vee's *diamonds* in my exotic wrist bezit was dancing under the lights, matched the Dub plus size rims hugging up against the 600 Benzerel, looking majestic like rubber bands on the feets. But wasn't even tilting the heads of those honey buns on Moet's frame. But the hell looked fine casting. And I'm posted right out front. Smell the knots. Fresh off the press like big faces, aroma of the finest Dolce-Gabbana scent, teeth starch-white rocking that Oasis

Colgate smile. No question, I wasn't excepting no for an answer, lecturing myself. Only if she knew where we could go, what I'd love to align those buffalo tender wings with. Got me biting on my lips right now, doing everything I knew of. Just wishing on us making eye contacts. Asking isn't not a felony, waiving upon cuffing in the towel. If it's heaven sent ! I maintain to believe real love hold its own sets of penalties. Have heart, follows da' money. "Say love," as I approached Moet. She quickly snapped her neck while dancing to see who was creeping up on those Vicky Thongs, only to gaze at the knocks before oppositioning.

"I'm not in any mood right now.. maybe the rebound uh' work out?" She wasn't shutting the gates, thank God! Implying; I'm noticing you, but it's not the best of times. Before she could finish her thoughts I reached behind came out from the blind, placing a bundle of freshly red, pink and yellow long-sticks American beauty roses, which were purchased from the restrooms vendors bell cap. You know those dudes who be posted getting that extra dough. Upon placed into her arms, nothing she was abled to do other than stare, and blush. "Awe, thank you," she responded kindly. Every bit of her was capable right then getting the bittiness. I held, retaining my thoughts. "I apologize having looked the wrong ways in my initial approach introducing myself." I fought with my reasoning. "I ought no why.. No you're fine." Before she could object I wasn't letting up. Plus, she was Jawsn. The V-V's were dancing in the bracelet, bouncing off the florescent brights. Quickly I pulled over the sleeves from my polo sweater, trying to keep her from getting to frost bit, blinded from the hard street hustles of mines. "Well, I already seen it. What you hidin' it for now? That's uh' nice time piece, where's you know- the his and hers at?" Aliiht! I thought about it and held under to the reins. "Thank you, but it's just a little something." I decided to downplay my hand, not losing her interest in the same jab, but she wasn't nearly passive. "A little something can mean uh' whole lotta muffins." You better stay alert out here cause dudes now days uh' have you relaxed. It's happen for far less! I'm hipped, but yeah. I ought be bouncing like dat! "My bad. I apologize, but what did you say your names again hon'?"

"I didn't, but I prefer "Maxwell" that works for you?"

"you mean like give you money?" She went in full frantic state. "You mean as in liquid from the banks!" obviously she heard what she wanted, but okay. How you getting at me, like dat?" "No it's nothing wrong, but it's unusual, slightly different, I'm kinda shocked you brought that up. I believe that I overheard something about the artist "Beyond" playing on KMEL (that's the Bay Area hip-hop number one station), his latest joint was featured for the first time on the air, soonest we were pulling into the lots, my friends noticed the track, but isn't "Goapele" and I heard the artist I believe Beyond they suppose to be performing at the

Grammy's next month. That Beyond's new single "Off
The Dribble."You heard it yet"

"Sure haven't. But I heard about it." Gathering Moet
had a musical bite on her, I debated whether not to
undisguised or just letting her gon' run wild on her own
inferences. But somethings are hard to ignore, and she
was just brisky like dat. I couldn't foresee losing this
opportunity scoring that lottery. My Maxwell instincts
vigorously made its way underneath the surfs. Like kinda
how science arguably is ahead of money. She looks to
sense the whether. And me having her best interest, as I
assured her. However, whenever- she could lean on me.
Before the approach settled in I feed off instincts.

"What might should I refer to you by love?"

Which, although I'd forgotten she'd already
previously given me her go to. While now I'm kicking
myself hoping she hadn't taken this outta context
meaning her business flyer she'd given me hadn't rocked
the attention span of mines, when infact that's what
it did, exactly! But I posted waiting anticipating her
response which mighta stun the both of us, but o'well.

"Um! I'm sorry hon' my answers Moet." I knew that.
Dang! how much sense was that. Anyhows these women
I'm meeting whether indirectly or not coming attached
to some kinda liquor beverage. Tequila, Daiquiri, and
cant forget our surest Moet. they'll like to argue some
of you men musta' missed the fax, but not! She had it

apparently right and under wraps. Figured out making her handle a dance of nature, rotating those high cheek bones dribbling the gifts her nanny musta fairly blessed on her. Beyond other than imaginations, daring you to look. I'm just sayin though, yet I proceeded on without deviating off script. Jabbin' and barking, playing for keeps.

"That's uh' stylish brief, it's fits you mighty well." I complimented just in general, I wanted for the life of me to give her part of my mind. But I didn't wanta overshadow the evening, so I pushed, holding my thoughts in check while at the same junctures I laid out my guided hand finding our ways outta distance off the jam packed dance floor. Her fingers were softer than velvet, which it hadn't help one bit whatever perfume she wore clearly stated a level of strength, courage and upmost confidence with pure dignity hoggin the traffic of our limited gapped space. As I pried us forward getting us outta dodge of harm's way. Once on the dance floor there were no more distractions. It felt supernatural releasing the anxiety that had built over the past few hours of our interactions leading up to a quivery exchange of more than just shiftable body languages. I advanced to initiate a softer tone, whispering.

"Perfection is only a blessing from God. I expect excellence so if by chance you find out through ways of mistakes it's me what's your heart wishes exploring, know there is not dishonor in happiness nor with surrendering." As Moet welcomed response was a treasure waiting it's avail potentials.

"Well, I enjoy that you happen over stood my position. Although, I have to admit over the years there's been unmet promises which produced more questions." "Other than wet dreams? Not saying' this is, but, if I appear unsurprised please don't' steer the opposite way, can we at least establish an open lines of communications?"

"No doubt," as I assured leaving my other sequences of thoughts drifting through midair to another suspense unspeakable then, yet I promised myself not to fumble, and kept on trimming away.

"How thoughtful and respectful. Most women woulda' just assumed my intentions were ungenuine. Then uh' get the nerve to be upset, when in fact it was their misdiagnosis of the situation affecting truly blessings of slippin' outta range. But you! I'll hold my contentions with. Another thing about you Max." I instantly flared. "What might that be?"

"You're very observative," and unapologetic, I posed. You must, but thank you. However, there's a couple hands fulls of you that I find overly flowing and some qualities you possess, which is unquestionably pragmatic, but in a good way." I've only known you every bit of two hours and you've got me eyeing and monitoring wedding dates." Which bounced right offa' me landing turkey-in plenty different ways.

"And uh' bunch of other women you've probably said the same too, sounds way much to be, but, Yeah alight. "I am listening hon. " As I appreciated her level of arrogance and sarcasm though, I ignored the bait unmoved while leaving the value on the table of what it could be. Respectfully poured out my reprimand of essence. "Do I appear confused?" Of course. Yet, I maintained. Upheld the growl, kept talking my shit!

"But I'll watch if you wanta dance fo' it." She hiked one hand on her hips and plucked out her wavy natural curly hair to insinuate, quit Jawsn. And blasted.

"I would say- none that's only assuming you'd care- then again I'mm consider we're being transparent. I probably could fathom someone, not quite sexy as you." Moet gracefully minded the fact. "No, no! I'm okay having you notice the truth – just I'm asking that you not deviate or mishandle satisfaction. At the same notions lifting uh' hand aiming two fingers to her eyewear's. We der', I followed, gotcha! Feeding the same, letting her know I'm not playing, but it's how she pressed her line kinda' drew uh' broader physical attraction upon me. As I have a mean taste for women who's assure of they knocks, and on they nickels (*toes.*) handling they business.

"You know Moet, with da' majority of these ladies I've bumped into hasn't possessed what's required inducing me to speak my mind these days. Am I alarmed? Probably not! Although I've discovered a difference about you from the rest, it's your perseverance and style that I find stunning, how you move about and that ghetto swag! I cain't quite place fully the thoughts how you dance.

"That's not sayin' much."

"But, did you know that most women often find sexiness through reversed ways of preference?" Anxiously she picks out I noticed. Opposite attracts that's nothing new.

"And I'm not speaking only the actual physical forms, but you unbother me as a person who scopes life quest from, the lenses with broadest discretions that's often misunderstood; but that's another subject for a better opportunity that you may need further clarity might "if" you're ready? Her affection it's deliciously threatening. I blushed within while caressing my thoughts. "That's what's up." My eyes aired, but I wasn't quite satisfied how my response fleeted out. Instead I lead. " Which from uh' women of your caliber it means way more." Had to apprise the taste of her wisdom with open arms, but still it was another side of the game she wanted exposed to, but didn't honestly know how to inquire those routes. I inferred without certainty from personal experiences. "A hustler by profession, solider of obligations, the gift of gab, square from the heart yet, with no dulled edges, born to answer." Looks if she read my mind- cuz how she feed in stares.

"Yep, hold those thoughts uh' minute, keep an eye on my drink. I'll be right back. I'mm let my friends know I'm in good company before they get nervous." As Moet turned leaving to this day I'm asking myself who painted those, Jeans-on-those-thighs good lord. It oughta been against the law for her to been stacked like dat. I instantly made uh' bee line surveying throughout the entire dance floor, praying not ah' sole was monitoring how my eyes had superglued attached to her motions.

I knew in just a matter hours our boundaries would become diminished. Her hospitable no's to yes's for the better sake likewise, held our positions from the other party goers. "Moet" promptly returned in the wink of uh' vibe, by then I'd almost ran outta act right fluid. The dance floor was yelling "Have you lost your damn mind Max." Not even! To the bar I dipped, who could resist the opportunity toasting at this hometown function hosted under the worlds famous visiting "N.Y.C" New York City "D.J. Flex." You had to been Overdosing on T.H.C. we partied like it was 1999. Packed like ground beef, bumpers ta' bumper still insisting on any reasons possible to own the evening. The bartenders were freely showing needed love which only enhanced the fuel to rev' the energy amongst us mushed party participates, and it was wa-y more google eyes than what was needed. Hands shackled tightly by boo bonic exotic thighs, nothing on earth coulda' explained the atmosphere as it begun looking more wetter and rewarding than the San Francisco O'Farrell's titty bars events, versus a birthday bash. But who was complaining! As the dance floor itself was drunk sweating up a storm. It's amazing how two turntables, and a microphone Sparks crowds, with old school jams of the early 80' procures, for get it. It Raises tight skirts high as the sky watches even higher. For the best parts Ol' DJ Flex's performance shut it down for the town, and particularly for dudes with little bit none, to acute's conversations whatsoever, found action. Your typical dime pieces were lax and approachable as the free drinks hadn't hurt one bit. I gotta own that– although it was more than just your stock weekends high profiles event. This was Jason Kidd's birthday bash. Every hoopster on the N.B.A.'s roster and they mamas were up rocking in the building, and it would be uncivilized not to mention us hood ghetto celebrities. We proved further than local views, it was money still in our ghetto's. I myself was doing the damn – Thang! While pretending as if I weren't dancing alone, "Precious" from the hood hit uh' quick glance before she noticed and immediately made waves, damn!   Right as I'm getting into the groove and the flow of thangz she wanta stomp on my parade. Just as the effects form the liquor had kicked fully in gear and here she comes pushing her fine sexy Azz right between where these other two notches I just finished shooting my shot with. A super bad, nodded seconds ago, "It's good hon', got you we rocking, be ready to electric slide up outta this joint." Soonest her other few Ponta's quit fishing. She was just assuring upon whether not I heard her correctly. Our non verbal conversation was way vivid. As I gleamed.

"Yep. I'm speaking ta' you – you couldn't wait?" Now I be damn! Tripped me the hell out, and I'm posted right there with da' both of my hands inside the cookie jar, overloaded galore with so much twerk, twerk, work!! Almost didn't know how to finesse outta da' joint, lying wouldn't of help one bit. Just luckily the two notches paid "Miss. Precious" no mind thankfully; and she continued on just ah' tootin and poppin' that thang on up in da' air like it wasn't anybody's eyes watchin' other than mines. And you know who was right dialed middle front and center. "Who?" know dat! Maxwell, blitz like uh' quarterback tryna get something to hold on with 37-24-36 worthy more than just my attention. They could of feed a smorgasbord full of starving bums on any given holiday. It was way too much on speed dial to been looking to broadcast, I wilded out! One of Miss Precious ponta's got at me like uh' "Maxwell- let me ask you uh' question in privacy real quick?" First thing arrived at my mind was I wonder what kinda' time she about to be on dick, dope or dynamite." She's not my women for starters. Plus, I'm not the one who spent off, that was a decision of hers to depart our wonderful conversation leaving her armpiece at a pool sight packed with nothing other than runway model potentials. But I learnt how to distance the barter upon

Omega's and my famously frenzy over landing that Lamborghini gifted from "Delishis Gap." That's not even considering the thirty bands, which was off the flux's- of the drip nah' mean! It was nothing. Although, I kept it on moving forward pasted eyes conditioned on the prize, despite any modifiers I answered surely. "Do you, I ought mind." Not that I hadn't realized the life's reshaping mishaps, I chalked it up as another eye opener from a treasured error. What you thought I'm, suppose to dip out leaving those two fine butter pecan honeys dancing unattended without responses. That's what wasn't about to happen. I instead quizzed for a sensible gist, leaving it up to the ladies they fashioned a solution, women are amazing aren't they, and blessed. They danced about and the looks of it, could of cared less, while gladly they twerked overtime hurting my eyes and the rest of the spectators, "Moet" she returned and the looks of hers appeared she was jealous, but for what, I couldn't answer that nor had the slightest intent. She was peeling it backwards-n-frontwards.

"You something else aren't you Mr. Maxwell?"

"There you go drawing conclusions." I opted, while denying."

"Don't you dare, try'd lie, I've been standing there watching you and those raggedy punk rocks."

"Punk rocks, As I barked paraphrasing admittedly surprised having missed out what Moet's eyes zoomed attuned, thinking I musta' fell uh' daze letting it dance right past me, as Moet countered,

"So you into fireworks like that, don't lie?" Which kinda' hit uh' nerve. And I differed. General' ral' speakn.

"Look! you got me twisted if you thinking I'm forfeiting, I ought do the fired cream love."

Talk quick not slick it's margin that's on the line.

CHAPTER

12

There wasn't any question Moet's intentions of intent begun revealing itself without any hidden agendas. I posed upon her the need for us excusing ourselves from the distractions. Now mind you I'm high as a dozen of eskimos flying ten kites on a Miami beach ocean sight drive. Further, we deserved some elbow room being in our presence alone. Quite playing who wouldn't agree our precious time better was us outta the way, nothing other just us, minding ours. As Moet, she took a second look before the opportunity even presented itself, I couldn't say anything extra. She like ta' caused more than just me to forfeit the other half of my phrases, prompting.

"Are you asking what I think you are?" Suit yourself take dat however you pleases which was only a suggestion. A better setting was more appropriate and retreatful for us to fully better acquainted ourselves, it was unplausible a more causal keynote warranted. You know offa' the radar type of vibe, but it was by choice not force, hands off no prints, wider dipps – what's next. She responded insinuating having read between the lines, but probably she couldn't have analyzed correctly if she thought what was inferred in nature only consisted sexual favors and or motivated by the likes of, It's quite obvious we resided on the same planet, but thousands of miles apart. Our ten seconds of silence was erupted by you wouldn't of understood.

"Maxwell?"

"What's up." As I eagerly followed up. Moet struck.

"I insist not going home to my babies with my back pockets touching." Outta thin air! That raised a mysterious thought. And I'm fighting now upon holding my dignity from spilling every which way but loose, which in retrospect's I acted as if I hadn't heard what she propositioned at least right then. I doubted whether not her thoughts were a little taken outta context. But didn't pay it much attention.

"So what's da' skit?" meaning what's Poppin'. But she just laughs tryna spin our conversation into the opposite directions before she begun talking out the side of her teeth's, the responses lead.

"You know, it's not that I'm saying you, but people can wrongly be stereotyped and mislead not paying closely attention to the undertones, fine tunes." I feigned but kicked out, "You mean the blush notes." Which my comments appeared to have agitated her.. Hell I ought see how, but she had to known that I wasn't being insincere nor ridding no huffy, she peeped out the handles I'm certain. Knew beyond speculations what uh' dude was flirting. Got me, now I'm thinking to myself, Maxwell keep it "P.I." *"Particularly interesting."* Let's not get sidetracked hold the reins Max, and avoid being that easily targeted one for prey. Cause wasn't Moet getting into my thoughts, I asked myself.

Know dat. Yup, I ain't gon' lie. When unplanned things happens our human senses take ahold, even while we're forming our next unfamiliar thoughts but something about Moet, goosh! She was a breath of fresh air and life waiting for exhaling.

"Please let's not get caught with our pants down."

"Huh. And by whom she gushes." I looked around givin' my survey, like as if it only was just the two of us alone, yet knowing I'm fishing. But far from starving for uh' bite of any dense bait, it was my way of holding her obsessions at bay. She vises.

"Don't think because we've shared a couple drinks and honest looks that I'm supposed to surrender what's behind the door number one." Her gestures appeared to in itself implied a broader scale, but I declined to bite. Playing my cards for keeps holding tight the hand to the nest as the four levels requires.

"Wait, wait, wait! You kinda doing uh' bunch jumping the gun lil mama, calm yo 'self down." I fired back. "I ain't looking to impose upon you, or anything you have going! Although, our opinions differed with one another's, yet momentarily we agreed but only to disagree on one thing in particular, and you noticed!

Hitting up Atlanta Georgia, but I wasn't about to let nothing derail with my goals of introducing her to that other side of life, whereas intuitions haunts and the grass desirably gets watered. One of the A.T.L's upmost finest spots. Bouncing tities, asses, jiggling, went blasting throughout my mind- and more tendencies than enough for floating the boat on shipping my brand new Lamborghini down South. And just yesterday increased my options mounting some fresh BB's rims exclusives, the big boy skates with Pirellis hugging tightly for handling the sharpest relays. Moet interrupts, "You know Max, let me share lil something with you hon." Her voice dropped a notch or two octaves. The tone which a mother sternly uses to admonish a child who's violated her directive orders, which was obvious she was getting in her feelings. But I listen while she opened the door for welcoming opportunities to be unfolded. "See don't think for a second I'm not looking to score uh' touchdown; cause ho-ney boom! You know I hardly can wait pouring you uh' shot, but I am required by the women of me for practicing self-discipline. And no, it's not simply done, but some of us we still believe! But I'll let you know this much."

"OK, what?" Quickly I answered not holding many punches. No questions my full senses were alarmed. I instantly yanked the thoughts about to escape. The situation was beginning to look utterly promising, but I wasn't stressing, nor desired pushed the envelope. Damn, if I do, and if I don't – right! But of notice it's mandatory not to discount the volatiles. "A close hand and mouth bound not to get fed." Here's my digits." I offered in contrary. I went for withdrawing my pen outta my back pocket, before collecting my thoughts. What in the hell ! I paused. "Naw, let's us fair exchange our ring tones," not that I didn't' trust she'd get with me, but it's America, and gingerbreads known even to have lashes. Moet smiled. Which signed, it's about to get deep. "Maxwell, did I pronounce that right ? please lets do not get on the offensive, but quite frankly I'm opposed to given out my phone number-just to anybody I haven't well vetted, peoples I'm unfamiliar with. Cause for single lifestyle women it can get thick out here. But I'll give you uh' ring."

"Uh' what, uh' ring?" I asked myself. You meaning like. Never mind! Do you. I figured holding my comments would only better suit and serve the both of us. Although, it wasn't outta the rims, my vision was nondistorted.

"That ri-ght there, that's exactly what I'm not indulging with, given you my number and you keepin' yours uh' Victoria. I hinted. That's further than the slippery fair trades and slopes, this wasn't anything like uh' trap-n-fade. Which even though. Kinda I'm most comfortable with; she powered forward on.

"If I give you mines, than I mightiest wells give you my address, and phone digits. Now ain't that bout' sumtin! I could almost keep not from bursting out laughing in tears. How dared she had the nerves perceiving her information was more superior than uh' plyers that's not fair exchange, I heard the hell outta that. For decades women somehow has managed getting away doing exactly that, now they think it's the gospel ways of life. But not today she's got her plate full tryna' school Maxwell.

Several hours lapsed I aspired to win the day as it neared our time to biniad that's ghetto terms for "flossin." Everybody's racing for the parking lot getting feisty for prime front looting space, which is right out front, for high siding catching bait and it was ghe-tto! And there's nothing more outdated than uh' lot full of parking lot pimpin' going on. Okay, I'm *Jawsn* cause you seen me leading da' parade effectuated off the stares from the twerk- And if your wifey says she wasn't, let her know Maxwell bets "whatever." And she's lying saying otherwise, but you know how it gets clubbin' past da' A.M. hours.

Meanwhile, I'm just posted out front politicking in my bro' Network's new drop 600SL doing my thug thizzal observing. And in the far corner outta my blind side uh' lil suburb chick whom I couldn't keep my eyes off in da' club was working it out something vigorously and I'm doing my damnest not to lose track of my next potential. Say dat then. It's amazing how women slides you those sassy, but classy enticing tendered glossy looks like, listen! Now if you don't bring – you sexy-azz-over-here-damit-right-now! You'z about to make uh' bee sting! Yeah, that's when you know you've reached that Louis Vuitton model's attention. I assumed she read my next moves, but I didn't take it for granted. I went further the distance, just enough enabling to fully enlighten her inquires of what my proposition may glimmer. Not to vocal, but who says you had to motto tone to express yourself. My actions danced like rules of conduct effectively stating in responses, parasailing out there.

"Only if you knew the things love we could welcome. Um!" Which irritated me dizzy, reasons likely; she hadn't adequately understood how best responding on Maxwell wishes, I haled. But, I believed she had, by the hand motions of hers proceeded our friendly non-verbal communications. "You talking to me?" What's up, yeah, I'm hollering at you the side kick, the one in those silky tight black-ish pants. As I motioned her in absence spoken words. Just as this heffa' Miss Precious whom I hadn't quite recognized, maybe because of how her chucky-da-donk-da-donk was busting outta the seams of those D.K.N.Y Jeans while she was way far to busy in Ol' "Flex's" options. Who's flavors had the whole dance floor hyperventilating. But you know something, without those beauty prong moles on her facial features, kinda mighta not even noticed who she was. It was ferociously thick, and I mean flooded with good work! No, I wasn't da' least bit tryna' biniad on "Flex." It's just I almost knew scoping even afar distance those hips on her had to much over bit, then Maxwell not to have something to do with. You wouldn't wanta bet that. But I goaded myself only for the time being. Luckily, which my actions appeared to went unnoticed. But it was afterourz of reckless eye browsing her full figured liberals truths, which stood well stock in my presences. It's no illusion she deserved and owned permission sitting any place near or within range of me that's not excluding the body-n-mind and soul for any amounts of time she pleases. While even thinking about it right now, it's by far crazy sexy and it's not to untaboo. I'm only implying and applying as honesty holds, if that's to much for T.V and America's audience, it's okay I do not apologize! Hate to acknowledge, nor do I intend to denounce otherwise. As I'd prefer not to hide the fax, than to lie on myself. Truth of matters honorably she's outside of providing any explanations on those very logistic- of their own. Nor speaking in circles outta sequences. Why lie on a person, when da' truth about that person may already be far savvy enough! Just given you something to wrestle with sorta' ta' speak. As I abstained slide her the dial you know things which nearly forces ladies hidden smiles. Then often departs without suggestions, "Real Trill" the kinda likeness you'd be watching, but still you find yourself tangled without questions, not looking for any direct answers and BAM! There's your breakfast on wheels bed site, without doubt it's uh' huge difference, holds more potentials when outta nowhere some complete stranger just got through brighten out your whole wrist, not to mention if the diamonds in the bracelet looks every bit of Wittelsbach'ish, if you hattin' you might outta let somebody get the rebounds, if not it's ok some of our feelings aren't easily shattered. But be sure to lap for the boards okay. Ooops! kinda like forgot your horns blowing up right now. If It's to much for T.V , get with me on the down strike cause right now looks if someone's adrenalines up, It's your time ta' shine Just a couple quick free floating thoughts dancing through. But it wouldn't hurt a soul learning what's on our to do list. It's aliiht, never mind. You ain't gotta' pay me no mind.

"Is everything aliiht Maxwell?" you've gotten mighty quite on me." Who wouldn't; although I pretended as if nothing was wrong, but I wanted to ask a thousand and one questions but instead just disregarded and simply inquired.

"What's with you? You some kind of famous movie star everybody's got sociable wrap at you. But I didn't go there, assuming that woulda' been too far fetch like losing my religion. Players don't negotiate the

xfactors, it's preferred aiming the keyless alarms toward the vipers and convertible phantom coups. Voluntarily qualifies uh' hundred percent of Miss. choose's attention. Our exit was manifestly made to the valet, whip was posted waiting sitting on deck as Moet parked one hand on her hip, bow legged stood. Upon, I nearly lost my mind, buckled like a cowboy during his rodeo, whose functions were for producing nothing other than total satisfactions. Riding like uh' thoroughbred outta this world, providing pure joy and smiles once reaching the finish line. "Aliith look-it you Maxwell, which I'm not about to even front. Gotta give you your props, nice set of wheels you pushin', matches you to the tee." As I fought the smiles. "But not quite as you though." I dialed non threaten, perfect pitch. Strike one, as I held my count for no other apparent reasons, only keepin Moet overly cautious of her *next unspoken thoughts* which expedited our ways forward. She had no idea brah Network and myself had swapped vehicles for the event this evening. But who cared. Had she probably peeped out the "Lambo" she woulda' been struck anyhows., But it was none of hers and most for certainly anybody's other business both our tendencies expressed that kinda mutual interest for one another. "Thoughts of wonder" which in retrospect's, neutralized any per se` jabbins of me searching out to learn Moet's real identity. I knew it was not likely Moet. As my actions hinted, "It's your world lil mama, gon' and bust uh' move." Bet, I'mm float bout it. She gazes with so much to smile about, in which who couldn't found her overly encouraging. But I wasn't about to overexpose and instead pressed on instant grandeur, thinking along the lines placing our opportunities splashing out. Finding the time later on during the "thirty-third" down the roads. You know dat strictly thermometer to bypass the hinting's of interest, while not stuntin' on the thighs, but pitching broadly. "Talk *quick*, not slick, it's *margin* that's on the line." These adventures I've learned from experiences at times rocks harder than initial push-ups, not always that's the reasons you stay ready. You ain't gotta get petty. But there's a tune society love dancing about, unlike decades before. Yet, although this evolution does has its upz and downs, those factors are sorta' depending on who you're asking. It's a basis of one's eye shadow.

But for now it's my time to glow as I rightfully unscripted without saying. I mightiest well splurge with a taste of conceitedness and arrogance, besides I almost can guarantee she thought I either pushed here on these Kenneth's or hitch-hiked; not that my conversation or dress code wasn't registering throwing up "King, and Steph" numbers calmly. Betcha she got that fax! Which attaches to the broadest senses. Far as I'm concerned I'm the best thing ever stepped through the zones arena, hands down at any sides of the triangle you dividing from. It is what it is. Profile six feet in half inches, early youthful, the American dream. One hundred ninety pounds raw lean muscle six pack abs, chizzed up, strong enough for building uh' house with only five hours of sleep per day, in sixty. Not to underscore the Oscar award winning Denzel Washington smile. Which matched my African caramel dark butterscotch's complexion and that's before speaking commas on the table. Nah, I'm not Jawsn – just letting you know, never am I avoiding the debate. Please; like the for real Gibeau Jean kitted out type, runway potentials and known to hit up Wells Fargo, withdraw uh' few hundred bands in "new faces" just for the hell of it- to glance the reactions on the tellers features yelling mildly like – what's your propensity Mr. Quick Cash "We knowing the grit holds its own dialogues, likewise body languages that laughs out loud! Reflective someone who knows how to work it out with rice sticks, reads general street love novels, working towards uh' formal doctrine or Princeton Law degree, a preppie suit and tie guy, carries a briefcase, six figure stress, b-boyz traits, bathe under tattoos, rocks french braids- but stay kitted with da' latest authentic spots attire/gear, forever on host, tuned into the latest hip-hops ghetto ebonics which is that the kind who does it for you? Then why not consume. You know exactly how to dial and manage the sparks where our hearts and minds resides, that's at least for integrals. Hands down can we not agree you are not alone having determined options of ours. You're not overlooked nor underscored on the boards, granted! America has it's agendas that I agree to disagree with Its observable wounds. A nation steered of non-patriotics with uh' few angry politicians at times it's only a crash waiting for paramedics and hospitals on overflows. Listen! Where's our blessed policy makers interests. Ignoring Our Angela Bassett's, Janet Jackson's, Mary J. Blige's State of the ark our Goldberg savages. Those aren't out of synce opinions, but intrigued instrumental pairs of visions. Visit the score. Despite, what if the streets raised few our perspectives and rightfully may have! And. Noted, as American's, times have evolved. Get use to us the likes of our next Serena and Vee Williams' our diamonds in the rough! The worlds become evasive, paying homage for our brighter days in whole. We've lived for learning, "some." But others- *okay*. And if we could have urges doing things differently. And, it's a modern fashion with a traditional twist, but I do love those ways of ourz. And Moet oughta understood the fortunate enough, blessed with a champion's bloodline, enabling the average beyond symphonies while some find this likely upon a troubling tangible, even that's kinda mind-boggling. Suffice worthy a closer look. She too found my persona hard to disagree, unwilling to ignore. You know the type: sexy bald faded, handles hood money well, forever jealous of his realness and God knows what in you, talks that street jargon curses makes love like uh' rock star. Your hoods roughest up around the edges, trophy-entertaining type, at every glance you find yourself getting thirsty given the opportunity to steal uh' peek and taste. You might swine dive without looking back- Yup! Armed to the tee with amazing bed and board room credentials even though we're the last thing searched over tha' internets, misunderstood, wouldn't you dare. But it's aliiht. It's those life skills and urban philosophy poppin swiftly outta the wits, probably what makes *him* attractive. Perhaps! It's okay if it's unspecified, love us how we come. Am I talking bout the ones mamas always looked twice at but warned and admonished you to hide the goods, which it's "whenever" likely she's around? But, aren't those the very instances if she dialed you, but you were outta' range- with extra radars near distances. Perking before you were abled "even" to be reached! Aren't those the lids, holding their own stare downs to those dangerously perfectly manicured feet's. Which bee's peeking outta' the fronts "whatever" kinda' expensive six-inch heels pumped, and braced onto the ankles exploiting plenty innocent mens looks. Um, I mighta' proposed, how lovely. But it's obvious who drifted without losing sight of the objective; of scoring more than just a leasure dance! As I nodded with my flourishing intentions. Like y' your eyes keep avoiding mines love. She didn't have any reasons other than ensuring herself- because there wasn't more needed observing. My mind was already made up, her actions had spoke absent any cushions airing, inferring.

"Believe you, I do have relentless pride with every glimpse and step taken in my lifes dance. And please have the decency to know before vamping opening and entering a divas world. Because bowguarding your way through hon', it'll leave you standin' out in da' cold and it's no need for you to heed my directions if it's pouring down in hail drops. Why shouldn't I maintain these bragging rights making only queen moves. Look, you may be privy whereas' only a chosen few have wondered, it's likely because you've protected your unquestionable place of gourmet. And no, I'm not wildin' out as they'd love to assume and say. just if you hadn't known "ah' piece of heaven it's fit for uh' king."

As I prayed the gates were not shackled. "Come here quit walking away ignoring me love, you know hearts fragile." Not that I'm' naïve, just I adored tha assortment of flavor she was bringing to the table vigorously, while yearning independently our options. But just uh' flaunting how she was ready to subject what was causing us delaying our moves at sea. Believe though such a golden opportunity of minding her, I overstood wasn't gonna be obtained beacon snapchatting. As I veered placing my mind inhabited on another course but damn! Thinking out loud she whaled. While capturing my thoughts. Moet she outta nowhere erupts like she tends to do regularly, maybe not on purpose. Suggesting, "Max, I'mm follow you or you following me?" How rhetorical of a question, I gushed underneath. Musta' been something other besides brew Ski Jaded in the drinks, that's when I valued the vessel done exactly what it was purchased to do. Stopping traffic like uh' boss leaning through on those Lorenzo's BB's limited sports, the deepest superbly dishes and kitted out! I announced half-heartedly after my brief recess from one of my *luxurious thoughts*. Although, non-advertised, but the vibes were soundly aligned. Climax, sex- and money! But never do I agree to those orderings, I'm opposed. It's not a trait for a hustlers mind frame to be engaged, with plans residing in vaults. Cause everything about her compelled nothing other than the scents about mints, and I'm not speaking life savers. "First alert me where we're going?" Moet graciously foxes out, still primarily avoiding the question. "It's been yo' world you know I'm just admiring." I vowed, she rebounded.

"You've been doing quite fantastic thus far, why shouldn't you keep on leading the way?" I Crusaded on. "You ever heard the term 'ghost riddin' the whip?'" leaving her kinda scavenging for hints, but on my P's and Que's!

"No, although that sounds mighty interesting, maybe not though." Yet I maintained my paranoia despite, she had me near the verge of exploding and I couldn't wait for initiations of her next tester-knee-jerking measures of hope.

"Boy please, you's uh' mess you know that don't you." Moet begun sucking on those juicy treasurable lips of hers drenched in some kinda Mac's gloss which laid perfectly on top of a pair of the prettiest features I've ever examined, which appeared uh' life time, plus. As I acknowledge she raises more than just eyebrows and at uh' time or two, but you know, it's not the beauty it's the duty and even lil mamas' non-responses like ta' caused a dude to wreck shop. Leaving me choking on my own opinions like uh' Jolly Ran Rancher. I'm not gon' lie, to be real my flirtatious visuals were sailing lost in da' moments, zoning out on her cantaloupes languages. Which she fought hardly concealing outta' my sight, but it didn't' prevent much, she had the Twilight Zone poppin' like *Dr. Jekyll-n-Mr Hyde* with mouths dropping, nonstop clientele. Like on a different level, with a stir. And summ' sassy but crafty-how she bounces. "OMG" upright and her position I prayed desired being with Max alone. Boy you not listing, it was. "I'm interested in whatever you tryna get into. You like hip-hop, bet- come on we about to put Maxwell everywhere you suppose ta' be, on toppa' da charts. Had me revisiting old thoughts how Omega and myself was making worldwide outta state plays on the highways. But one contention I hadn't wanted misplacing, could she hold and sustain throughout the roughest weathers? That's the question. Which im not knowing. Yet she knew and spoke the same languages of clout. Something which is non purchasable and it differentiates the rules of life to a degree. That's what I admired about "Delishis Gap." She was ahead the averages bops, it wasn't solely about gettin' Parmesan "money." Noticeably she was mindful and moving under the soil getting her nails dirty, her foot works patent spoke for itself, and to this day I cain't unwrap my thoughts how she dribbled that Lamborghini out to the hoods trenches, was astonishing. Her preference and solely appeared introducing Maxwell Pixar into the finer things about life, as achieved. Got me still wondering about the likes of somebody like, Nah. That'll kinda be to optional, who probably wouldn't speak or explore a healthy conversation if wedding dialogs wasn't apart of the equations. Which, who am I to be pre-judgmental regarding. But I'mm lean outta the way- ways, as if most men who's bright thoughts may never eye dribble another desirable women, maybe stoops- once bowing onto one knee, and guess who I'm looking for? Which no Lamborghini or money bag is worthy its' risk what's in front of my eye lids. Those there hips pealing outta those seams at heart on lil mama Moet, look uh' there! You better quit playing we need to be   vamponing. (meaning getting someplace.) Yesterday. Leaving this Twilight Zone scenery. Yeah, I know you heard me!

Not much of distinct in the world abled to stop what's of existence.

CHAPTER

13

As they say nine tenths of the law is possession, I'm tryna find out. Moet she has me relatively asking myself the savoring questions how did we get to this level of the game already. She's pulling up into the Waterfront High Rises in Midtown San Francisco right underneath the Ocean's Pier. Perfect viewings of the Bay Area's richest lifestyles. There's boats traveling in and out, docking from statewide which is daily inbounds for tourist attractions and those who chooses for shopping at the finest places. And the food on shore, justifies its own surnames. It is mindless how good it taste. Just as I'm speaking we're prowling into the buildings tarmac front gated keyless entrance. Security guards patrolling out front as if we're approaching a secluded neighborhood for nothing other than multi-millionaires like uh' Paris Hilton Chic. Now these are the triumph joints, they've been known to run at least ten mill' that's just the starting prices it's not uh' blip below. There's nothing low maintenance about even having the thoughts of say owning an inch of a square foot around these views. As I pioneered in thought, she gotta' be doing something extra besides bartending. Still though I felt some kind of ways inquiring, just sorta' didn't think there was any room to ask, but certainly was I curious. "Off the Dribble." Stock they fully equipped with Olympic-size pools, fitness rooms, work out gyms on every floor, underground parking and shopping, you know the works. But still, in my mind I'm wrestling within— not to be to nosey, didn't wanta jeopardize that number one draft picks opportunity to share uh' piece of my time at her. Not that I hadn't qualified for the look, which she rightfully earned and over qualifies the gaze, and some. Ok! Now, why am I trippin for? Hell, I wouldn't know. I'm kinda surprised the thoughts had even circled my mind, but like the average young gun of my youth- in my shoes; promise you, he'd eye hawked the same way. Like "did we just arrive here at heaven." It was marble and gold encrusted everywhere. We found our way through her parking lot, which looked more of a city in itself. The bellman was prompt, ready offering his undivided assistance looking around the specters of luxury; I filtered. "As he should." Welcome and how may I assist you today Miss Moet?" He stared with a smile which spelled. "You're one hellva lucky young man. Hope you know dat!" Almost but. "Thank you, I'm enjoying the helping hands that's before ours." Her surprise response felt as if I just graduated from an ivy league's university, stepped my game up – few notches letting the truth speak for itself. Then I pulled out my hoods geek ghetto card-well said. Which comes first nature upon a boss, but it was like walking and counting money at the same times as if you were floating through the world on octane. She answers, "My pleasure." Escorting us, lifting her arms to insinuate, keep straight ahead. "Moet" instructed like she was use to the standards of given, versus taken orders and red carpets being rolled out to her anytime she entered her exercise living domains. I noticed there was an admirable restaurant food court right out front the entrance on the second floor. "Kirby's Food Bar and Grills." The smell of Cajun Oriental tropical flavors came whispering at my taste buds. Which we know Maxwell's appraised at value, over his good sesame chicken and shrimp chow Mein. And yes, I've had the opportunity to indulge with Zen. And let me just say this- the endorphins of pleasures can rock the bastes world, leaving a person sound to sleep. You'll get up the next morning "optional," but it's like breakfast in bed on wheels. I followed. But why she hadn't alerted her plate ahead of time.

"She bee's getting it in hustling under the radar. "How lovely I aired." Noticing how she thinks, has me kinda amazed. I knew she couldn't ignore how well we fitted from the first time our eyes flirted, my whole world did uh' one eighty take, the other half of the equation she possessed. And I wouldn't of had it no other way. "When, where or how." Damn! if she'd let me only figure that out. Yeah, simply thinking as she radiated leading us into her lavish spread. Lil mama she woke up my scents game.

"What's wrong?"

"Nothing! Just minding our business." She laughs.

"Our business." I caught myself glued to her ridiculous frame, and not just the body, but in mind too. She was wet and smoother than a Gillette razor shave.

"Seriously Maxwell." Absolutely believe dat! And I meant she could get the bitness' beyond imaginations, which she held and answered back through her incredible stare down gaze, for real. I can't assume beginning to sit and assess exactly what she'd meant. But it felt heart wrenching. Am I in over my heels profoundly. As I mumbled only to myself, underneath my breath. But that didn't stop her from leaning on.

"Yeah, you in the presence of a real women ready to give you uh' run for your money hon.'" Moet conjured floating out there stopping me from fishing what I almost landed her way. I glanced over my shoulder and stole uh' peek of her bending over grabbing her house slippers from underneath her plushed out leather turquoise sofa. Um! That spread on those thighs-outta been against the law. She's about to make uh' dude go nuts! I survived not to say. "Damn, you working da' hell outta those Versace Jeans, you think they worthy uh' break?' But I couldn't picture letting her slide without fifteen minutes of prancing around under the well lighten living room lights. Then she slide in those Spandex, oh Lord, now it's just out there, indifferent of those looks from inside the disco. At least She had a shirt covering over the bacon, now it's just fully exposed," and it's to much to watch." But I'm holding my cool, as my eyes are having a field day, lap dancing. "How nice of her. And she frowns before dribbling. " I never try to work backwards or in reverse." As meaning, once leaving the job sight it's uh wrap. But I differed. "Moet" she knew how to split her day job with personal activities of life – quite well. It was obvious, I recon'd she hardly viewed herself the windows of multiple opportunities, for what possess dudes of my caliber acting this way. But I downplayed how much she was affecting my innocence of ready to throw in the towel. Like luckily, there weren't any jewelers open at the hour, they'd been a half of million richer. I mighta' broke the bank draining my life's entire savings and took my chances for whatever she had favor of me down on one knee. She had become an instant drug of my choice which my heart had prayed for, she blushes.

"Does it matter what I decide to wear inside?" Are you- am I making you uncomfortable hon'?"

"Seriously?" I feed her the looks of wonder. Why lie. What, um! "What I have on doesn't suit the hour?" it wasn't as much the things she feed, but if you were not there to have envisioned the gaze, you would not have the enjoyment of sharing my taste.

Getta grip Maxwell, don't let her dictate the show I pressed myself. But did leave the table of shrimp. I faded her- but just say, lets bet she acknowledged the work

"I mean, I'm use to hour glassy shapes, but I'm finding yours somewhat more distractive." She kinda' smiled and laughed to herself. Hinting if maybe the liquid fluid had taken its toll on the evening, and I coulda' had possibly one to many drinks. I glanced over to study my watch and it said a quarter to three. But there was not uh' more desirable place to be besides sight seeking under Moet's prances. And it was notable to the both of us, her and myself. "Hold on I'mm be right back." She dipped outta sight into her master bedroom. As I believed she was re-rocking her fit into something more unrevealing. How she'd cheesed at me, appeared she knew her beauty was wearing on my nerves. That's me tryna' to avoid uh' refusal her perfect figure spreaded over the couch. Yet, I viewed as equal satisfying, but was my partial response of two adults just doing thangs "OTD ?" Within minutes I noticed the shower was on and I instantly grinned. That's uh' wonderful ace! She dips out drippin wet, "Did I take to long?" She whispered seeking to almost been unheard in a lower baritone of voice. Anyhows, I kinda' of just assumed she was speaking to me. "What. Did I miss something?" Moet pretended she hadn't said the first initial words loudly enough. Although, she was utterly clear.

And I woulda' responded, but I think it woulda'been a mistake. As my honor was watching Moet lotioning her body right in front of my eyelids with a bathrobe, half opened showing nothing other than those vulgarly interesting hips. She tried to hide probably asking herself, "why am I torturing this young man, he doesn't nearly deserves this." I hungrily stared enticing her to not stop while purring beneath the bathrobe ensuing purely imaginations, coulda' rocked worlds offa' the glares.

"Let me ask you something Maxwell." Yeah? I zapped, quicker than she had the time of rethinking, had she thought twice of switching her mind up. "What if I said I'm anxious to learn the reasons your eyes hasn't stop frisking on me since our conversations at the Twilight Zone." She could not in hind sites solely thought of blaming that on me. Although, I wondered if she'd insist otherwise.

"Why you say that?" But I quickly changed subjects to another topic. Instead, figuring why leave room for the debate.

"What's that flavor perfume you were rocking in the club?" I inquired.

"Moet's Passion."

She acknowledged as I felt her eyes dancing between my legs. Luring closer near the edge of the sofa towards my directions.

"Why, so you can splurge with my ingredients on the next chick." She launches.

"Nah, I'm just asking. But it would make a perfect anniversary gift."

I bargained. But she didn't bite.

"That's the reasons exactly right there, that I'm not sharing my secrets they're exclusively for me to know and other hoes to envy!"

She rolled her eyes at me like she couldn't resist had I proposed right then. She didn't know it, but I hadn't thought twice loves enabled upon first sights.   Until maybe uh' few hours ago.

"And no I'm not saying that to ring any spontaneous bells, but don't worry I'm not tryna' trap you." She growls, warmly. Appeared, she read me like uh' physic mind physician with exquisite credentials in heart science. Cause sincerely that's what my perplexed intentions consisted of. I searched the sky and said a prayer, "Lord if only you would somehow honor this one wish, I'd be da' luckiest man alive. But the line of questioning didn't stop. "I gather this is your happiest place on earth, that's if you don't' much mind me askin'?"

"No, you're fine. Let's just say it's my come as I need to get away bungalow." Bungalow, I caught myself repeating after her, but not on purpose. She had that legitimate effect, that I couldn't know how to recount out loud. But it was nothing to underscore with.

"It's nice and cozy. But yeah." She pauses and then answers. "You mighest well say it's home!" Almost like she had more to say- but reserved without going further.

"Quite frankly."

"Then what's da' big butting for, are you– thinking about it or have other looks?" As I kinda reversed the handle. Sorta on my fishing expedition risk.

"Nothing in particular." While she answered this round of inquiry stiffly and dry. I felt her eyes stalking my inner soul for their own answers outside of what I mighta' had the typical rebound for. But I invoked my gamblers card, exchanged equal glares. Kept it P.I (Particularly interesting.) Maybe because at the time kinda' experiencing da' moments of my life, to busy observing her knocks from the freshly scent of whatever body wash she'd reappeared in, holding my attention at bay! But in the same notions my eyes engaged receiving an unforgettable grand stare. Her palace was plushed-out from the entrance floor gold plated pipings down to the kitchen's marble door handles. The views overlooked the San Francisco Golden Gate Bridge. Yeah, I'm puzzled now like bingo, done hit the lotto Maxwell! Only thing absent the his and hers keyless entry, and it's cookies. (official) The hell if she was booked yesterday, spoken for those thoughts rung as mud under the waves. Lil mama could easily noticed whomever; she's rerouted her pace on moves complimenting her perks, issuing marching papers. Not now ! Yet, better right now! Whatever plans use to be on the table homey can get reacquainted with inferences- cause you do not-owe-uh' soul any explanations. Not how she's fox trotting got me over working, swiping these eye lids. Please believe that! And I'm dearly wit da' pose. And if I'm uh' day late, still uh' hour on time ahead of schedule, far as I plead.

"Aye this damn view is not making any sense. The sights from where we visioning it's fucking offa-the rails. And it's uh' full moon. Your brights on love? "Are you looking over there at those stars compounding da' skies?" As I motioned utilizing my two Vee' peace fingers, the sign language often hit up by Pharrell Williams, which reflects his Virginia Beach Maryland set. I veered towards the Bay Bridge's city lifestyles, which she was more than over arousing my interest. Moet she crept like butter calories on me, and now I'm feeling her prying right through me without motioning in the least bits. Then those Sexy Azz pair of hazel brown eyes, um! Good Lord-y. She clutches both of her hands on her hips pouncing, switching her entire body language, proudly from one leg to the other. You know that high powered conceited good pussy-talk, hourglass stance, when you know a person's eyes browsing you like uh' hungry German Shepherd just drooling, foaming out da' mouth. And she's bouncing that undismissable look~ before she feeds.

"If I decide to give you a sample can you even handle a shot?" Now mind you maybe she's just uh' few years my senior. I'll give her that. I only believe this because looking above her living rooms mantle appears that she holds uh' bachelor's degree from Spelman College outta Atlanta Georgia; it just registers with my "Maxwell" senses that she understands life beyond bar tending, and probably utilized the *Twilight Zone's* atmosphere as a hustler's tool to better position herself amongst the elite. Who can argue at that. A glance looking like every bit of a pick-of-da-month clean outta the Jet's magazine. Meanwhile, softly relinquishing that treasured stare, examining thoroughly over my entire features before speaking nonverbal, insinuating Ho-ney, you have no idea the gifts that I'd love to share with you. The greatest of which life has to offer, but you not paying attention, or are you. You must cain't see put some glasses on hon' and get with me. Quit cheating yo'self playing. Just the thoughts of her stance alone paraded.

"Just answer this one question, what do you think you graphics about the full moon's Maxwell?" Right then and there Lord knows that I coulda' eaten the buttons offa' her pants, but I didn't' need her thinking of me solely the lawnmower type of guy in a hurry to trim the weeds. Almost I dared, but I didn't bother— that woulda been greedy. I know huh! Yup, as a thirsty bicyclists who just got finished riding like uh' bat outta hell, I opted of ultra-religiously distracting myself placing us on a more solid and neutral ground, but she-was-edible! Then I answered slowly tryna' not to lose tha' disposition to amplifying.

"Everything you think that I wouldn't, on any given day, if you's ever somewhat apart of such equation." Aliiht! And you know she pretended not paying attention. Selectively focusing. And I'm trying not to growl loudly sounding like uh' cub lion waiting so innocently to be petted. Sho' nuff I musta' dialed good money she went berserk! I cautioned myself. Stay focus kay Max. She's in expendable you're not in a hurry, it's a marathon not a sprint. And she had the nerve to ask outta nowhere. "Have you ever had a mystique situation as this via your personal sought assistance upon a woman's desires with specific fantasies?" At my initial instances I'm freaked right, how open and honest she peeked. But, I wasn't surprised, considering it's not a women on earth that I know of who doesn't have a taste of freak underneath. And Moet she reached her intolerable boiling degrees respectfully, but was it something I done or may haven't said to induce or influence her. Which I'm not ashamed of the *lush* in spite even had it traveled over my head. But o'well – it's not the first time a pair of panties came landing on my lap, but I'm praying she's the last, sincerely following losing Omega. But I'll depart with a smile, but never again. As there's nothing about her, even had I wanted, I couldn't disagreed with. She had complete handles on our destinations, I introduced let's try dancing to a different tune and see how well you manage with misbehaving, as I urged. There's when I discerned her third eye came aboard the whims of her facial features lit up like traffic lights. Her mascara had found it's places everywhere within a dream of mines. Bed sheets, pillows, and mattress, touching nearly everything within a twelve foot radius- putting it mildly. Like we were at the WWF wrestling match. Upon impulses badly had I wanted letting loose to say, "We ain't lap dancing get off my lap." But I didn't go there, held my thoughts for the rebounds. Noticing that woulda been unorthodox putting da' cart before the radar.

"Hold tight – wait ah' sec. Let me grab something." Immediately my hood senses light kicked into tactical alert mode.

Oh-man, lets hope she's not going to get what I think. But I quickly disregarded those thoughts, overlooking the Bay bridges perfectly comfy views out of her luxurious penthouse spread. When she returned in hand she flaunted with some good ol' save the day Kay`y-jelly. I'm like aliiht. Bet right on. Yup, yup! Quiet down cakes up. "I thought to myself," then inferred. Let me find out you some psychic mind reader for real though. She had that lo-key smile about herself the

Jewels possessed of a runway model's behavior. She was unlike any I've encountered over the years getting ready for nurture. I could almost sustain from smiling aloud. She hits me with something total outta the ordinary. "It's only evident the type of assistance you may be requiring – that I would only think you run into plenty, reluctant gaggers quit regularly, or am I your first?" Ok-ay she wit' da' shit I fought. Lashing out not knowing whether if that was a tsunami shot or a blessing in the skies, tasted like bait, not knowing though had I made the wrong assessments of her, but she wasn't at ease. Should I kept on wearing my hopes for high stakes out loud? I phrased. "Didn't you not say you had plenty mouths extra you needed feeding at home, or was I zooning to hard offa' margaritas?" She begun sorta mesmerizing her thoughts in mind, it looked troubling for her to express what was dancing through her visions. Yet, She recounted, but with an array of charming stares. Looked probably if her uniform she was about to slide on mighta' been clashing with other forms of reality. I only loitered that out there to get a reaction, on how well she perceived life. "You have nothing to worry about. It's only me." Upon I lead.

As I looked out towards the oceans views, "Thank you Lord!" cause her valuable assets hadn't appeared the furthest conformed under those work ethics. But I coulda been wrong. As I focused on course which is a traditions of the four levels the game prescribes, with obligations if you're playing for keeps. As I entertained those notions. "That's that sugar daddy talk." I heard what she likely meant about to almost ruin the evening, could she be getting in over her rockers, but still I'm popping it. "Haven't anybody taught you about quizzing a player?" She lashes out, with promising sets of observables looks – partly reluctance before she darts.

"What is that! if you mind me not asking?" she pretended as If she was born yesterday, tryna' gauge out my intent without us clashing.

"Just fetching ain't cheatin' do what you do lil mama." Although I wasn't willing on risking the rewards venting, while she posted legs crossed, massaging her fingernails through my tender scalp. And that right there bo-y! Betcha' know exactly what my cheers about and my reasons for dialing. Maybe somebody does anyhows, I wasn't about to pour gas on this foreseeable vault those thoughts disappeared just quickly and starkly as they entered the radar!

She filtered out one of those sexy as looks, it takes two to tango simulations. But outright; I'd chosen not to envy, cause she was capable of getting the bitness! But it wasn't up to me. Whew! It was like nah. Love this ain't gon' work, you know the sayin' if it won't, dance and tik tok with it, just relax and let it flow. But to avoid complications which maybe she was just ahead of herself. I asked how many drinks had she consumed- but didn't get uh' response, felt as if something other had her actions preventing our explore. But You know how it's consensual with words out a persons mouth, but the body language having a different conversation. Like – uh', I ought think so. "Yeah" that next level of the game, but not quit having the words. One can not make those kinda faces up, but if you's uh' goer; it's in the heart, you'll make something happen. Her eyes leaps out of her fo'head leaving that drippy lobster taste on the table and in more places, other than one of the six nature senses. I wish I knew how to say it out loud, but nothing was getting in our ways of reaching victory. Imagine that !

Now looking to finish what we started hours ago, shifting into a more gutters approach, yet neutral zone. "You never struck me the type leaving anything as much of what you wanted unspoken for." Now we jawsn, could had I possibly made an error of misjudgment, insisting on keeping the boards lit. But I peeped how quick things veered south, and I kinda sorta disregarded those notions. Until !

"Maxwell, I apologize."

"For what?" Got me snapping like uh' Rottweiler who's not eating since the past few weeks. As tears begun to rinse down Moet's cheeks, I knew it was late, but not that late. Well !

"What's wrong?" As I made the room for her to explain herself without feeling under to much pressure.

As the right thing to do, I notice. Leaving the gap open for score.

"Aliiht I'll let you know sooner than later."

"What?" I sharply probed. Not having any ideas of her not having divulged the reasons of her being so teary.

"Stop crying and speak what's on your mind love cause right now I'm not comprehending anything you're saying." Then out of thin air "Moet" fesses.

"You know Max." "What?"

"I'm a virgin."

Damn!! how paramount might this be those are the only thoughts which orbited through *my mind*. No she didn't just say what I believed!

Gotta stay mindful!

CHAPTER

14

Summertime and it's California sunshine boy taste the runways they're viciously swell, enviously delicious, and some. As I'm admiring sportin' a clean look through the frames latched onto my facial from a limited edition pair of Beyond's eye wears recently to graze Nordstrom's rack shelves about uh' month ago. I haven't seen anybody rocking these joints. I could of died simply peeking over its pricey sticker. They knocking fools over the helmets for two bands, damn! That's kind of an expensive taste for a pairs of eye wears, but they fitted just as pleasing on my features. Right what I needed for a bright Sunday afternoon. So I flossed uh' tad-bit leaning through the hood on Dub-pluses, big boy skates twenty six inches on da' cleeks hurting the feelings. Those the kind be prepared of coughing up every bit of a rubber band per wheel. Don't pop uh' tire out there spinning playing to hard. I'm hipped nor try fronting on anything under, not round here on these escapades you'd become yesterday's conversations wishing You had spent candidly- pissed, and hardly abled to digest you were cheating yourself like dat, knowing well you were outta' pocket and needed coughing up few extra biscuits in order to untwine correctly. Ladies these days are dominating the valve and letting dudes know relentlessly, "I expect a certain measure of noise you thinking about distracting my attention." Although some honestly got the nerve to suggest the world for a player, but not prepared going the distance. Ain't that hood for you.

I'm babysitting the leafs, just out minding my own not bothering a soul enjoying the fresh air got my personal shot of Patron doing ghetto Maxwell Pixar, you know thangs money does. The hoods done gotten way obnoxious outta hand everybody wanta' play captin and golten. I believe that's the wrong perspectives and I've got the right- maybe to stay in my own lane without agitating the slopes. That's what I hope, primary reasons I'mm not the least bothered. Focused with my dividends and the hell on the drama. After last weekend getting Moet's google eyes has redirected my skates, and rerocked my inferences of what's even qualifying to enter these realms. And I'm fully content about it.

The Daytona Beach Spring bling it's approaching noticing it's about to be prime for whaling a piece or better. But you reel in a bite on those boards you would wanta' bring out the rice and aisle, not owes!

Those bikini wears are nothing to second guess with, be prepared for throwing in the towels. You miss that ride leaving the stations; you'll be kicking yourself for decades, which It's a mistake that I measured the year before and haven't forgiven myself todate. Kinda came blind sided as it wasn't something written into the four levels the typical rituals. But it's obvious if you engage you best always bring your G-14

A-game to any arenas cause reality hands down, it's for keeps *"talk is cheap!"* It's hard not to suggest if you lose one opportunity you forfeit the options to regain the reins. But without a queen on the boards, life could be drastic. But, stay hopeful, optimistic and a contender for the trophy. I believe there's not much of distincts to stop what's of preexistence.

"France hit me the other day and ensured he was cleared for our travel. But, it wasn't without uh' fight having had to drill his parole officer on many different instances. Likely he's upset for having confined to monitor the work in those thongs from a distance on T.V screens. And you know, it's going be on every social media outlet, news, talk shows and more. Bra Network's in, and the other homies have given verbal consensus. It's about to be packed out, and the rarest breeds planet earth has ever seen, it's gon' up and I ain't sparing not even the proper pronunciations, nor leaving the room but to score! Those gifts out there be coming handpicked, it looks. But you know something, I'm not going there!

Up bright and early today as always. About to dip in on my lil moma "Omega" not to get mushy-mushy just peeping out the agenda that's on our business partner slate. Which I'm okay enjoying her as only a part of the Vouge Tires Ent. Platforms, it's platonic. She's taught a dude a thang or two on life's particulars, it's more than just one-way breaking bread. You must maintain an open minded position, often has rewards which may require a person of exercising opinions, not feelings and be present for obtaining the whole parts. It's formal neutral mathematics, but she and I continue with a respectable bond, it's not simple being single and up and around the likewise kind- a precious diamond and not having the urge to Jawz at it. But, I'm kinda' skeptical with my glances of course, damn right! I'm only human. And she "teases the hell out of my nerves." How is that? Because of her beauty it's the kinda' love and prejudice which yells-like to good to be. Yet I'm not interested overestimating the dial, you know women picks up vibes in a heartbeat whenever it "even" appears there's' any threaten opportunities of their positions. But she doesn't have anything to worry at, not that we share any moral obligations for dating anymore. Shit I prized dat on the Lamborghini. Ask me whether I care, probably not much as I should. But if she was in my shoes you think she'd be losing any sleep? "Exactly." She would wanta respect the effort. And these splendid ideas, we do have and share the same vision with. But that "Delishis Gap," that was a once of a lifetime and I can't blame the facts on her. But I'm not looking to dispute the results, nor the least upset over. But I'm not gon' lie, just thinking outside of my mind it's enticing having the hues of "the yellow sky" brushing up against you from an old love. Someone who's even as excited as you are about maybe uh' second chance. Busting lap dances around your taste buds on a regular basis. It almost get's miserable honestly. I'm like please, quit teasing my mind. And she buffers with inflictions, encouraging slants, which aren't minus the vaguest drips of what's perking at her thoughts. And she has that good good! But we don't go there. And I'm not doing anything minus interfering her contentions. "Otherwise" knowing her, likely she'd hit that tactical alert zone, sending her antennas into digital "H.D mode," and you mightest well forget formulating running any plays outside of that. It's finding yourself speaking to her Kay Cole hand from outta the hood. "Implying," boy-bye syndrome! Which are likely her invariable grounds. Cause everything becomes under the subjectives of scrutiny. The sketchy part, it's often gossip from the haters anyhow who were plotting your position from the start. Which I'm more devoted having toast to the best things life has to offer, they should muster how. Instead of being bitter putting on fake smiles that's easily detectable a thousand miles before you even close enough saying the simplest as "hi." I often wonder about individuals with a heart to despise, that's gotta be difficult to look yourself in the eyes at. Knowing how you vision the world around you, it's determinative of pain you're abled of causing another human for no particulars, which makes you proud. But, do I agree.? There's things about each of us deserving of airing out. It kinda helps you to avoid that extra load hauling of another person's baggage often invading with achieving your blessings, predominantly no one's perfect. Considering. I've learned to forgive, but not forget. There's actions I have acknowledged to respect whether right or wrong for the better, probably not on purpose as these written forms of spirituals may be founded in the purest forms delivered in the hands of those who may even despise love, fear and hate daily around the globes for no apparent reasons under the sun. Damn, for real though. Regardless, I'mm pace on. You stay committed. I'm forever jealous of my realness. I wonder about how they gon' love dat! Wishful, I am of those who may insist they overstood this individual Maxwell Pixar, and that's uh' good thang. Know I'm unshiftable on this never ending journey to invite plenty from my best of friends to those who even appear nonsocible thank you too. Know the sooner our hearts are rightfully appraised, assumed in whole as the worlds' concerned- our untelescopable and misdiagnosis for the foreseeable likely will continue without pauses. One stepping forward and two in opposite while not leading to any significances of real values for change. Finding that hidden smile often, isn't a citrus fruit it's beyond the root. I have no misinferences of realities that there exist an unspoken agenda. You need not ask twice whether not my thoughts futile. But I'm honored each day having the opportunity to at very least, achieve a smile. Plenty cannot say the same.

Noticing how God gives his hardest battles to the strongest of his warriors, often they question their quest too at times, forgetting to focus on the rebounds. I've found intimacy to endure life's traveled maps, though I've become surprised of the unknowns. Despite, still even while working with cloudiness, I'm amazed. Then again I'm not, how life presents one's detours. But, I'm mindful not to fear nor panic. Which it's helped determining more than just the readiness. As I'm bracing for the bumps, yet I haven't ignored other foot steps around, nearly impossible to avoid. But I'm posted listening for that inner quieter knock, that may likewise need to look no further. Knowing what a person's desiring could very be staring between their own presence, and in some ways more willing uh' spar. You said it, maybe one day. Until then, I'm content of just acknowledging the thoughts.

Hearts understood– must be love.

CHAPTER

15

I'm home busting down in my work-out space when I heard my cell phone ringing offa' the hook. I answered on the second ring. Picks up.

"Hello?" Although, kinda busy, but I answers only to say, "Let me dial you right back." My blood was pumping, sweaty and itching. But the other party didn't respond. Okay, I looked. Who's playing with me now, taking dis ol' precious needed time outta my daily routine work out. As I just was about to get off the horn, I heard the warmest flux. It was "Delishis Gap" speaking, but sounded like she was drinking tears. "What's wrong love?" Which now I'm alarmed! "I just cry for no reasons, quit walking away from me love." And then she hung up the receiver. I'm posted looking like-did she just say what I think she had. How about now I'm over intrigued. Questioning had I known how to betterly detect, except and or understood certain unfeed things more vividly. Maybe would not had underscored what brought out such painful reverences. No one had never done anything to me as rewarding, having such an effect- that drawn my attention makin' me alert to entertain the search of my reflections, for what coulda' sparked her actions. It was different.

Her number hadn't appeared on my phone's log ID, almost didn't answer. But something out of the ordinary kinda made those decisions at the time- elevating the situation of me answering the horn. Which now I'm about to lose the screws attached to my Vogue Tires. As I pictured and tasted her tears through the dial. There was no doubts about it in my mind "Omega" and probably "Moet" too had some formal knowledge what was going on amongst us. It's the vibes they relinquished which caused a reaction. I cain't explain how my heart surrenders for yearning their intentions of intuitions anytime our thoughts links to this day. It's our bond of trust which speaks underneath my soul, it's that knee deep. Almost like a conspiracy hidden theory kinda' twang. Which only I presume, but I'm not about to grasp nor deny. Yet, it's hunting! Yeah that kind. And then these latest wave of events, a trend on Tik-Tok some ol' internet site, which until "Omega Star" and "Moet" raised the idea via in a text message about some dance, before that, I hadn't even heard of such app. And only within say an hour ago. I visited their site for the first time. And if you mist, I am computer ignorant!

Which is only my fair assumptions if you might. As I have the slightest clues about internet surfing the web. Other than Myspace checking for updated post or DM's. "I'm-ghetto-huh!" Yeah, I know. I be late on everything just about. At least that's what my younger siblings would want me believing. But you know better than I do. That's only to follow someone whom I have disagreed to except their friends request. Well, I'm at the limit they've only given what five thousand spaces. And I'm leaving the few that are open for guests who?

"Bet you would wanta' know!" Say anything you won't about Maxwell, but you not gon' weigh I'm late for a lunch. My nieces and nephews they always having attutidues tryna' school Unk on the latest trends what's moving and grooving and lately they've even got tired of responding to my messages. I've just written it off as that's teenager's world of flossin' where once you surpass twenty one you sorta old news and vetted out. Lil of they know that Unk's active and paying attention. Enjoys keeping up on the latest trends. But anyhows, I be on their heels teasing and they getta kick out of me tryna' be thinking I'm hipped and superfly. And my baby niece she's growing at a pace of intelligence, anytime she hears I'm near, it brings out the brightest of her treasured smile. But I'm tickled how they laugh so hard at me; that I refuse even to listen. And as I'm speaking, I just looked over my pager was on overflow messages, which read an invitation to sign up under Tik-Tok- yeah, I didn't know you had to have an invitation.

Goes to show how much I know about tha' internet-ok-ay! Then the unsequestered text messages I'm getting these days urging that I join the search for Delishis Gap vs. Maxwell Pixar under the "first dance" you know I hurried up and tapped the letters in. Although I didn't quit- kinda know how to utilize the app, until my nephew "Aswad" show'd me what and how to find the dance, and I couldn't stop watching. It's populated with content flying across the globe. There was an old photograph of me leaning through the hood in my ferocious Porsche and I'm givin' it up banggin out the roof top. Mac Dre's "To Hard for the fuckin' radio" which was our hoods function track back way when. My instructions from Aswad on exploring the Tik-Tok dances were followed to the tee. As it panned out smoothly there was a heatwave of fluttered excitedness whomever clicked onto the links.

Pop-ups of swarming groups mainly exotic driven women and the dancing they attuned in sequences looked they'd gotten schooled from analyzing Luke 2 Live Crew's footage; "but the underground versions." Grooving and bouncing dat back, promotional slogans on

t-shirts which revealed the worldwide search for "Delishis Gap and Maxwell Pixar" was rapidly exceeding anything I understood to wrap my thoughts around. And in unisons, dominating the social media platforms utilizing phrases like "Delishis Valentine

Knocks, Maxwell Off The Dribble, I Dreamt heartz understood, Like no other, and Come on." The listings stretched on and on. The whole nation had on different hoodies,

t-shirts and in droves- kitted out dancing N-synced. But it's how they designed the apparels merchandise that differentiated, which did it with me. They had over a million subscribers. Champagne bottles popping cutting da' rugs looking sexy as they wanta' be. Which I'm gaining more and more confidences as I kept on watching, aligning her photo with mines. Like we were kissing making out. She appeared looking for me and likewise was I hunting for her. Which is kinda "L-7" (square) being she has my attention. Although, I do not have hers. Ain't this kinda ironic she happen texting me almost about an hour ago. But now we are on Tik-Tok, with a dance that's exploding viral. Millions of viewers are participating rooting for us to become a married couple. "Which must be love." That's gotta be one heck of an opera for the worlds' indulgences. As I peered with optimism whether or not a person's interest or desires having their inferences chaperoned. What if, she or I opposed of this Tik-Tok dance publicly gettin' hitched, as it's to late now- we're on full blast. And I mean it was widespread, our faces were splashed out on

t-shirts with catchy phrases and the regales matched our hidden smiles. It's nothing other in the world can prevent determination when it's heaven sent as ours appeared quite obvious- despite the outside looking in. I begun to wonder not, Moet or whomever were actively perpetuating with staging the Tik-Tok dance, kinda awkward how Moet played like she was a virgin the other day. likely testing how far I would fetch outside the relms or had my thirst for "Delishis Gap" stabilized enough not to risk losing her. But then again that logic did not fit. I hadn't made any particular advances in regards communicating such talks with Delishis of becoming groomed up. That's not to say, I wouldn't of disapproved. But on the other hand she kinda' hinted something to the neighborhoods after that rubber popped! And we've yet settled that score!

The Lamborghini and the thirty bands came before the sudden romance quite frankly, to think about it. But damn, she was Tik-Toking her Azz off though! Just thinking to myself. That's- wild. See and this one thing I'm finding caterpilling about most women. It's how they'll sit back and plot a move, already have an intended goal and they do very little talking implementing their approaches. But us men we be to relaxed out fishing at the disco's, we'll wait until the D.J announces last rounds for alcohol, then start that hurry up scrambling like cockroaches when da' lights come. Women, sitting back laughing at our unorganized asses. Honestly, it must requires a particular mind and skill set on spotting that right potential good to-go. Which in my defense ya' boy's getting better, Look how Moet and I slide out! Now that was uh' furious you peep. Maybe after another shot of Patron or Mia Tia, if I luck up catching "Delishis Gap" online at the right time on that Tik-Tok hype, betta look out, I'm at that! Although, I'm optimistic of the unanswered shockingly disappearances of hers. And she's changed her phone number and hasn't fully effectively reached out to me since those first interactions, which maybe she was respecting the fact of Omega's and I relationship. Whatever caused her to ignore her "IG" Instagram text, it feels way further than her needing time to herself. And I'm having a genuine doubt whether not Moet was even a virgin and utilized that as a tactic resourceful means of distractions, to avoid being rude and uncovering her real agenda. Not that she hadn't wanted, supposedly revealing her diamond. It's fair to infer from the attitude of hers, probably she knew something that I hadn't or just sorta' look the other way at. But there's a similar baseline that is very unease between conversations of Omega's and Moet. That's not just rhyme and reason, that I align to surmount with. I like to attribute their kindness as they've both displayed nothing other than mannerisms of that ol' wifey kinda' looks. Plus, Omega she's out there with it kinda thick, and planning on introducing me to other levels of the game, venturing with my Vouge Tires Ent. And she's foot working in traffic as a real women suppose to, matching her conversation with actions. But I wouldn't except anything other.

Our bond over the years it was, I wanta say — hood, but it's deserving of better language. Yet, the unconditionals, while since having met "Delishis Gap" and her bumping into my whip, further fully unleashing more than just its value. "She did the fool"! She went under the vaults and came out way savvy. That Lambo gift man, I ought even wanta' go there ! Damn right! My whole attitude towards interested in other women, it's become outta' character with my spiritual to look further upon sharing myself. I might look, but soonest it's time to get closer I am taking aback of how beautiful it feels inside. But on the outer surface although, I might appear approachable that's not even the dial. As it's known love has its own ways of showing up whether expected or not – and that's what's got me doven blindly. Delishis Gap, she's propelled a hold on me. And I've come within grips of recognizing which in posture appears Tik-Tok is one chapter and the others, I'll keep to myself. But it's not uh' part of my wishful list. Not Omega nor Moet neither could pry us apart. And they're both nothing to be overlooked. And no, I do not devalue our distance relations, it's more than just the verbals – and expressions. The range of her intuitives are louder than the unsaid, she overstood there was an unusual flame between "Delishis Gap" and myself that was bright shinning as the sun. Even still, her loyalty and love for the things we'd acquired together wouldn't' let her post in the ways of my happiness nor had she danced off until she knew for certain." I would be ok" happily and satisfied! That's when I discovered the real essence of what sincerely unfeathered beauty looked like. **Often** are the things unseen and said about ah' person which makes more of a difference keep dat in mind. Yeah that part!

Never try betting of what you not abled to loose!

CHAPTER

16

For whatever vague reasons I cain't get any sleep this evening as I'm often home during the daytime because Grannie she's getting old and needs me around the house to run errands and help her with Grandpa. It's his birthday in four days they suppose to be going to Reno or Las Vegas. Pops loves him some craps and Grannie she travels just to watch. She often fusses about how much he's betting outta the savings, but it doesn't bother Pops in the least bits. And plus, I heard Old Man has a mean strike. Knows how to stack the dice to hit the numbers he's looking for. But I doubt that! Yet, no one can rule it out, being somehow he finds the ways of winning, it's almost like the dice he uses are loaded with numbers predestined before out on the table, and in motion. I often asked him how does he win, is it luck or technique. His answers differed from theories in general, which often lands. "Never try betting what you can not afford losing." I discern that gambling wasn't foreplay. Which is how I begun to approach the game of life- chess. As others might review differently, it's food for thought! It hadn't swoop down on me until Omega's acrobatic moves and the warmth ways of hers that I begun viewing life through a pair of eyes undiluted inferences from a comfortable distance. Loving how she responded to the uncommon provisions of the street life. Had me observing with a more humbling vital mechanism how beauty can in itself have a radical tone, depending whether beauty's ones escape. Still women are uniquely seen way differently than most men, whether or not that's justifiably isn't my position to say. "As if money comes with instruction," or the same means of shapes. It's the rules of preferences which It's foolish of tryna hide the fax from yourself, it'll shine even at times of the darkest hourz. It's just dignity finds routes, gotta respect the facts. Omega she didn't feign after learning of my missteps, Instead she opted not to act outta repercussion, which in respects had I earned? but purely luck musta' saved me from heartbreaks. The reasons I believe silence weighs more of one's opinion. Omega she found solace because she had no jealously in whether not she gave her best efforts with making me happy. But some things aren't meant, others are heaven sent. I do not oppose.

Just the other day I'm looking over my bundles of mail, I happen running into a letter from the same realtor who'd written me almost six months ago tryna' sell me a loft. But this letter had an office address outta Midtown,

New York and I'm a city boy, born and breaded in the heart of East Oakland-worthy upon notice! Sometimes it's essential putting ya' show on the road. I kinda' just. Implied to myself paraphrased, man this gotta' be on another level. But, I happen questioning- maybe this the realtor whom I made friends online from Instagram, IG. We kinda' recently kept in contact over the weeks, maybe though months– but it couldn't been a year. As I opened the letter, which was addressed to: "Maxwell Pixar," from New York, NY. The sender Ten Dimension Energy Land Mind Petroleum, West 42nd Street. I begun the surveying the letters contents- it held my attention just by it's heading. "A Landmine was ready for fracking with plentiful Oils and Minerals." Now I'm fully drawn in, how in the world am I reportedly listed the Lessor. I keenly adhered out of suspicious dire, overly enthused as I immediately peeled into my rolodex's phone book for the attorney Mr. GoodWrench's number. Although it hadn't appeared criminal in substance, but I wasn't interested undermining my freedom, the light showed "Freedom first" which is our neighborhoods local bail bonds. You know I just got finished bringing that bid, outta Alameda County. I learnt my lessons, Vouge Tires Ent. we were just getting off the ground quite fabulously since Omega was overseeing marketing and promotions. Each release had mounted almost two hundred stacks and or better. That's not hurting for dough, and I'm veering investing in real estate, which might we contour looks promising; I'm getting the educational sponge out for the reaping the rewards for living the life of a lawfully abiding citizen plus, paying my debts to society fairly considering my actions. I landed the attorneys Mr. GoodWrench's number and gave ah' ring hopeful looking into procuring fundamentals on how I've acquired these landmines in my name. "OTD" (Off The Dribble.) Petroleum ready for fracking Oils and Minerals. I'm like wow! it was music to the soul. "Law Offices of GoodWrench and Sons, how may I be of assistance this evening?" The voice of a secretary announces her presence from the other end of the receiver.

"Yes, may I please speak with Mr. GoodWrench himself? Let him know it's an old client "Maxwell Pixar" and it's kinda urgent, might you. Thank you much." "My pleasure. "

As I waited for the attorney to answer the line as I continued examining the documents carefully from Ten Dimensions Energy Landmines thinking to myself, who in the world sent me these documents? This tasted like fried shrimp! I frowned at the unknowns.

"Hello, Attorney GoodWrench speaking, how may I be of assistance to you?"

"Mr. GoodWrench, it's Maxwell Pixar. I'm not in any trouble that I know of *shit*. I'm praying not. Listen, I just gotten a letter with a contract from a real estate agency implying I have some forms of property rights for a Landmine Petroleum, but it's unknown to me where and how I've acquired this. I'd like to have you research the substances of merits, I'll fax you the documents."

"Wait ah' minute, did you mention you have something from Ten-Dimensions Energy Landmines? My phones' going out, I almost can gather what you're asking." I felt the urgency tone through his voice, but stayed focused.

"Yeah that's right." As I assured him.

"It's Funny you reached out, as I just was about to give you formal heads up. Perfect of timing. I've just gotten a letter myself from their main headquarters office which is in Texas. They've requested me to reach out to you surrounding a potential limited amounts of Oil and Minerals which sits on thirty acres, flat-lands that's underway for fracking. How did you- well, let me rephrase that."

"Mr. GoodWrench wait, now how did they even know you represented me or knew of me that's kind awkward?" Yea, right! While our dialogue was more straight forward than it had appeared, he and I begun of reasoning. Well it's a notice that appears you make a reference of me on some kind of dating platform. "Yeah, that's right. You are there on my front page as my contact legal personal advisor. I make the references which in any regards of real-estate or other investments anything such related you're the best contact. And that's how."

"Go ahead." As Mr. GoodWrench suggested.

"No, I'm just saying, it's obvious you are the lessor that's on the title for this Landmine. it's a gold mine, you may have struck the lottery- if there's any potential merits for what I'm reviewing on your behalf. You've luckly may have scored big time! "

"No shit."

" I just was about to dial you right before you phoned. I wondered if you had any knowledge of such property, and any partners involved. Thinking maybe we could work something out." What an opportunity of goodwill. I probed! "Sir, I'm just learning of this today. Are you kidding me? Woooh, Molly, Holy! You mean you had no inference nor thoughts of how you've acquired this real estate?" the attorney Mr. GoodWrench was lost for words. As I urged.

"That is correct, how much would you say it's worth from first glance ?" Upon I quizzed. "That's ah' Good question, It depends on several key factors, but I'll conclude you may not need to hold any typical day jobs if you so chooses not anytime soon. I'm almost certain you'll be satisfied with pension residuals. Moreover, I have an legitimate offer, let me represent you throughout the negotiations of these ventures and I'll fully work on a contingency basis. Plus, I will promptly advance you a lump sum of cash in order to ease any stresses you may have going forward. How does ten million solid fit into the equations deposited wherever you like before noon today. Does that work for you? But its' contingency's based on if we can agree on two reliances." Mr. GoodWrench bargained, but the numbers caught ahold of my attention quickly. Ten mills; hell my thoughts were fully booked thereof.

"What might those be?" Quickly I attuned undivided attention, not letting Mr. GoodWrench initiate any second thoughts for reneging. But I feared I hadn't read the underlines, which could be jeopardizing the full values and or possibly surrendering portions of ownership rights. His offer nonetheless, held my interest saying the least, but I wanted further insights of the evaluations. Although, I didn't want to impose upon any consignment deals, nor with raising doubt surrounding his representations. Cause hell, he's talking about making a difference of me becoming a millionaire. Versus holding hands mashing plans. As this wasn't no fantasy perceptions. Within what an' hour that's the best shit I've heard of concert- I want to say my entire lifespan. The Lambo even wasn't on that level not that I'm ungrateful keeping the score, lil moma did-the-damn-thang! Fo' real, hands down. There wasn't much I needed learning for the better senses. The Land Mines were under my name, leaving no open spaces for further debates-coupled, Mr. GoodWrench's approvals. Hell, count Maxwell fully in. I noticed the actual spotting of the site and the lands positioning had reportly sat in Nashville TN, as I kept asking myself, but I wasn't abled to make of much sense of the whole ordeal. And I hadn't known anyone residing out there, Let alone had that kinda loot to buy uh' Land Mine for fracking Oils and Minerals. This danced through my thoughts nonstop repeatedly, but it had not deterred me from approaching the bank tellers window for inquiring on the largest amount I could have withdrawn on an instant notices. Now with Mr. GoodWrench on the analysis and his offer boy, it sounded very enticing urging upon my appetite. The teller stated thirty thousand if I provided at least twenty-four hours notices and seventy-two hours thereafter. It was no limitations with funding if the dough had been sitting and marinated for fourteen days or better. Leaving me speechless, planting multiple impressions into my thoughts, dripping with imaginations enough for provoking me with a mindful ungeniality. What in the world am I about to do moving through traffic with dat' kinda bag, but for sure wasn't studying any possibilities about any illegal hustling that was out of the questions. While dreaming in my sleep came about expanding with Delishis' family franchise. And I awoke noticing my phone light was beeping which meant there was unanswered text. I glanced through- it was none other than who I hoped for. "Delishis Gap." Her phone number for the first time was revealed, *UMM* look uh' hear! Instantly I went interalia, like how am I about to marquee this diamond. She was impressive at on every which angle you viewed her form. She was bright, smart, humorous, humbling, sexy and so human that I woulda forfeited to her the

Lamborghini and the stacks had she asked, including the thirty bands that she'd withdrawn for damaging my Porsche, during our fender bender. Looking over her text messages inpart read: "Maxwell, I'm not seeking to stir up your relationship with anybody. *Omega* nor *Moet*, but since our first exchange of smiles and that rubber popped! You have, or we've, re-aligned my entire life. There is a photograph attached of our bundles of joy, It's the gift of love, you have no obligations. Although, if you desire not, as I promised you upon we first spoke but what's *next* not what it once was, I apologize that I approached your ex- Omega. I felt it was my womenly duties. I found her on your "IG" social media platforms. Then we became good friends. That's how the Tik-Tok dance got started.

To Be Continued

BOOKS OUT AVAILABLE NOW
Visit and order on Amazon for our latest
books:

Off The Dribble
Swift Justice
BEYOND Worth Uh' Dance

By.

The Govenor

For bulk orders visit
https://www.urbanlifedistribution.com/

HOUSE REPS Publishing Presents

OFF THE DRIBBLE
A NOVEL

THE GOVENOR

Made in the USA
Columbia, SC
21 July 2022

63801988R00119